Sierra

Julia A. Royston

BK
ROYSTON
Publishing

BK Royston Publishing
P. O. Box 4321 | Jeffersonville, IN 47131
502-802-5385
http://www.bkroystonpublishing.com
bkroystonpublishing@gmail.com

Cover Design: Elite Cover Designs

ISBN-13: 978-1-955063-41-8

Printed in the United States of America

Dedication

To every young man or woman who is working hard, going to school and wants the degree, then the marriage, then the baby and a very successful life. Keep Going!

Acknowledgements

First, I acknowledge my Lord and Savior Jesus Christ for giving me all of my gifts and especially my gift to write His words.

My husband who is always supportive, loving and encouraging me to utilize all of my gifts and talents. Thank you honey.

To my mother, Dr. Daisy Foree, who is my number one cheerleader and always tells me, "hang in there, you can do it." To my father, Dr. Jack Foree, who is never far away from me in spirit or my heart. I only have to look in the mirror each day to see him.

To Rev. Claude and Mrs. Lillie Royston who support me in everything I do.

To the rest of my family, I love you and thank you for your prayers, support and love.

To the team of BK Royston Publishing and Royal Media and Publishing that make it easier for me to write and publish the books I love, thank you!

Table of Contents

Dedication iii

Acknowledgements v

Introduction ix

It Can Happen for Me 1

School 23

The Wrong Class 27

The Forced Group 35

Home in Winter 61

The Snowstorm 69

Back on the Road 79

Scandal 89

James 99

From Ignored to Observed 117

Dr. Sutton 151

Spring Break 155

The Conversation 159

Spring Semester a Senior 179

Spring Semester a Senior 195

He Granted Her Request 215

About the Author 217

More Books by this Author 218

Introduction

Sierra is a focused college student that has had a crush on Dexter for a long time. Dexter ignores Sierra and to him she is invisible and not worth his time. Even his mother reiterates the idea that he should not date anyone in his city or definitely not anyone that attends his father's megachurch in Cincinnati, Ohio. Sierra feels that she is destined to be by herself or just focus on her dream until a chance meeting with some friends over winter break with some friends and in walks James. Experience the joy and pain of love as can only been seen told by a young female college student named Sierra.

It Can Happen for Me

"If it happened for Ms. Jillian, it could happen for me," Sierra Campbell whispered to herself while standing on the New Life Christian Fellowship Church steps. The June breeze blew lightly as she watched the highly esteemed and popular Jillian Forrester, now Jillian Randolph, get in the car with her new husband, Byron Randolph, to go on their honeymoon and to start a new life with the love of her life by her side. Jillian Forrester Randolph was popular at Sierra's church as well as their church's organization. Sierra had watched 'Ms. Jillian', as she and all of the other teenage girls at New Life Christian Church affectionately called her, go from struggling college student to powerful entrepreneur. Ms. Jillian was the lead singer of the choir so Sierra would watch how she held the microphone and sang each song. She would go into her home basement on Sunday evenings and practice for hours, mimicking Ms. Jillian from earlier that day. Ms. Jillian was Sierra's role model and the one person besides her mother who she had really looked up to since she was born. She loved how Ms. Jillian was comfortable in the skin she was in. Sierra had never talked to Ms. Jillian about how fond she was of her, but she hoped to one day. Ms. Jillian was always nice to everyone. She spoke to all of the young girls at church and was a fun chaperone for the one Spring Break College tour she sponsored. Ms. Jillian wasn't a size 2 and neither was Sierra. Sierra was not extremely overweight at the age of 18 but, at a size 12, she was much larger than the size 2 through size 8 girls in her youth group. She was not as tall as her younger sister Kenya or blessed with her long, straight hair that hung low down her back. But, Sierra's five foot six frame was covered with caramel brown skin that got darker when kissed by the summer sun and naturally curly hair that was never touched by a relaxer or hot comb, thanks to her mother's softer curls, would do just fine. She knew that she should lose weight, but the doctor told her parents that she was healthy and should remain active. Sierra would take the body that she had been given by God until she got a new one in Heaven. The Campbell family consisted of four children and two loving parents. Sierra had one sister, Kenya, age 17 and a brother, Samuel Campbell, Jr. age 13, and her parents, Samuel Campbell, Sr. and Stephanie Campbell. Sierra was always proud to say that her parents were happily married, slept in the same bed and lived in the same house. Her parents were high school sweethearts, married for twenty years right out of college, and they argued sometimes but loved each other in spite of everything that had happened in their lives. Samuel Campbell was an accountant and Stephanie Campbell was a teacher in the public school system. With three kids, two dogs and an aquarium of fish, the Campbells had money struggles like everyone else, but they both worked hard night and day to make sure that all of the family's needs were met. Sierra was the oldest, but her mom always emphasized that she was not responsible for raising her siblings. Her mom always said, 'Sierra, your job is to enjoy your life as a kid first. One day you will grow up, get married and take care of your own children and not mine. These are my children but your brother and sisters.'

Sierra loved music, church activities and after school activities. She had been a Girl Scout, volunteered for everything at church that she could and was considered by some as a leader. Sierra had good grades, close friends, plenty of family and was cute, with long hair, beautiful eyes and a singing voice that could fill a room and move an auditorium of people to tears. She loved to sing and she felt wonderful each time she was on stage. She knew that she could sing well because people told her so after each performance.

Sierra Campbell was living a perfect life, right? Wrong? Sierra wanted what every teenage girl wants, to have a boyfriend like all of the other girls. She wasn't thinking about marriage at 18 because she still had to pick, attend and finish college. She just wanted popcorn and a movie every once in a while. Sierra had a date to the prom, a date to all of the homecoming and spring dances, but they always dumped her after the dance. As a matter of fact, she got dumped after or right before every season or holiday. Why? First, she wasn't easy, promiscuous, a naughty girl or whatever they called it these days. Second, she was crazy about a boy who didn't really know that she existed. He was standing on the bottom steps with the other junior groomsmen waving goodbye to the newly married couple. The junior groomsmen had been putting wedding gifts in Byron's black Escalade but stopped to say goodbye. His tux was still on, he stood six foot four, brown chocolate, and for an eighteen year old, he was beautiful. Of course, every girl at New Life Christian Church liked this particular boy and every girl's mother wanted their daughter to date this boy. Who is the boy? The ever handsome, Dexter Sanders, Jr.. Dexter is the son of Rev. Dr. Dexter and Mrs. Marjorie Sanders, Sr. who were the first family of New Life Christian Church. Dexter Sanders, Jr. was not only handsome, but intelligent, great manners, respectful and the most eligible teenage bachelor in all of the World Christian Fellowship Conference of churches. Furthermore, the mother of Dexter Sanders, Jr. or DJ, as he was called since a child, thought he should marry the prettiest, smartest and most wealthy girl in all of the world, not just at the church. His mother spoke often about how young people should strive to achieve, live and have the best that this world has to offer. Sierra realized that Mrs. Sanders wanted this for her son more than anyone else's child. Mrs. Sanders made sure that everyone knew that she had the best, finest, smartest, most handsome, most talented and future pastor of New Life Christian Church as her son. Mrs. Sanders was more than protective of her son; she was downright obsessed. What made it worse was that the Sanders' only had two children, one daughter and one son. Sierra's chances of marrying or even getting one date with the wonderful DJ were slim to none.

Dr. Sanders talked weekly about faith and that with just a little bit of faith, you could move a mountain. Sierra's faith was in God. She believed with all of her heart that she would date and marry DJ Sanders one day, but she surely didn't know how. She believed it more standing at Ms. Jillian's wedding because if Ms. Jillian got to marry the man of her dreams then why shouldn't Sierra marry the man of hers? But, this mountain was big, huge and gargantuan in Sierra's opinion. God could do it but would He do it? Sierra was convinced of her goal. Now she just had to convince DJ, his parents, her parents and, eventually, the world. How to do that she surely didn't know. All Sierra knew, in the voice of the older ladies at her church, 'this is a job for Jesus.'

"Sisi." It was Sierra younger sister, Kenya. Kenya was the tall, calm beauty in the family. She was five foot eight, long hair and a size eight. Sierra loved Kenya with all of her heart but oh, what it would be like to have a body like Kenya's.

"Huh?" Sierra answered, somewhat distracted.

"What are you staring at?" Kenya was looking down, turned her body quickly to get her face closer to Sierra's face to gaze in the same direction. Sierra slightly jumped back like a fly was flying toward her face and gave Kenya her full attention.

"Just watching Ms. Jillian leave to start her new life with Mr. Byron," answered Sierra in a very plain, monotone voice.

"No, you weren't. You had your eye on that Sanders boy, DJ." Well, her sister had caught her. Standing at the bottom of the steps, was DJ waving goodbye to the bride and groom as he closed the door of the limo. His parents were standing nearby as well to wish the newly married couple well. "When are you going to stop being obsessed with him and go on with your life?"

"I don't know. He is just so fine. I just wish I could have one chance with him."

"Really? I don't get what you see in him. He's arrogant, conceited and a mama's boy. He is not going to date, drive, be employed by or marry anybody his mama doesn't approve of," Kenya said convincingly. Kenya knew that Sierra had a mad crush on him and had for years. She also didn't think the DJ boy was worth spending the time of day with.

"You are right about that but, still. I think if I just keep hoping, I will get one chance to spend time with him and maybe start some type of relationship with him," Sierra said while deep down inside knowing that she didn't have a chance in the world with the great Dexter Sanders, Jr.

"What have Mama and Daddy always told us about relationships? That when it's right, it's right and you won't have to change yourself to be in a relationship with somebody," Kenya said.

"I know, but you have the body, hair and height that guys go after. You have never had a problem getting a date and you are just 17. I always end up dating the boy next door or Mr. Nice Guy who is so nice that he is boring as a pile of bricks. Don't forget all of those nerds who seem to come my way talking about neutrons and computer algorithms. Then there are also the Mr. Wild Men guys who just scare me by wanting to borrow money and feel like a bag of popcorn at the movies earns them the right to try to have sex with me. Heaven help me, but I just want a Mr. Wonderful. If he is good looking, career-minded, progressive, smart and has it going on, could be something thrown in too. Is that too much to ask? Can you feel me? What's wrong with me? You don't understand what it's like to be me because you are standing there gorgeous and have guys falling at your feet!" Sierra said through clenched teeth and held back a scream that was blaring in her head just knowing this fact. She loved her sister. She wasn't really jealous of Kenya per se, but that statement right there brought that green eyed monster to the forefront for the first time. Sierra felt that she didn't quite measure up to Kenya. Furthermore, even though Kenya was her younger sister, Sierra always thought that Kenya would probably get married before she did. Why she worried about this so much, she didn't really know. The Campbell's house rule was the females in the family must go to college, graduate and then get married. Sierra had four years of college before she would have to face the possibility of marriage so why was she stressing now? Maybe it was because they were at a wedding and the emotions surrounding this occasion were having an impact on Sierra as well.

"Stop it, big sister, right now. No, I don't know what it's like to be you. But I do know that I love who you are and what you look like right now. Don't change for anybody. You are smart, funny, pretty and got it going on, too. You're cute and thick, but you're not obese or have to even shop in the plus section so why are you looking at those toothpicks? Take a good look in the mirror sometime and not just the magazines. Find all of the right things about you instead of all of the bad things that to the right guy doesn't matter at all. There is a guy right now who will be worshipping at your feet and super glad to have you in his life. Don't overlook the Mr. Nice or Mr. Nerd, but please forget about the Mr. Wild Man. Don't stop living or keep trying to change yourself for some guy who will probably disappoint you in the end," Kenya pleaded.

"Kenya, how did you get so smart?" Sierra asked.

"I don't know, but you are smart too, so act like it. Wait on Mr. Wonderful and stop worrying about the Mr. 'doesn't know I'm alive'. You've got four years of college to go before you can even think about planning a wedding or getting married. You know the house rules."

Sierra gave a quick laugh as she listened to her younger sister. "You are right, Kenya; you are so right." Sierra was trying to keep an open mind as she listened to the wisdom of her younger sister. Kenya was right. Secretly, Sierra still wondered what it would be like to be with a guy like DJ. He was gorgeous, popular, suave and well-known in so many society circles. What would it be like, really?

"You ready to go?" Kenya asked Sierra but it was clear that she had gone back to dreamland. "Look at you. Stop daydreaming about him for a minute and come back to earth, girl."

"Leave me and my thoughts alone. I'm ready. Let's go find Mama and Daddy so we can go home."

Sierra and Kenya headed back into the church's Family Life Center to search for their mama who was one of the hostesses for the Randolph reception.

"Hey, girls, there you both are. Did you wave and see Ms. Jillian off?" Mrs. Campbell asked.

"Yes, Mama, we did. The car was a super stretch limo; they were beautiful and looked so happy." Sierra smiled as she recalled the scene. Kenya just remembered the look on Sierra's face as she stood watching that arrogant DJ.

"What did you think of it, Kenya?" her mother asked directly.

"I love Ms. Jillian and I am just so happy for her," Kenya said.

"Well, we are about to finish up here. I need a favor from you girls. The decorator had to leave early so we are going to have to take down the bows from the pews and various decorations from inside the sanctuary. Bring the bows, any ribbon and the runner back to the family life center. The candelabras and flowers along the pulpit should stay in the sanctuary. I will have your father get the candelabra off the pulpit and store it for pick up on Monday. The flowers are donated to the church for decoration and will stay until they start to die. If we hurry, we can get everything cleaned up, get home and go out for a movie and a pizza. How does that sound?"

"Great to me," said Sierra.

"Great to me too," said Kenya.

Kenya and Sierra walked to the sanctuary, using the back staircase instead of going all of the way around to the front entrance. Their intention was to come in from one of the side doors that was on the left and right off the bottom of the stage which held the pulpit, band area, podium and choir loft. When Kenya was just about to pull the left sanctuary door open for Sierra because she reached it first, they both heard voices in the sanctuary.

Kenya stopped and said, "Shush, I think I hear people talking in the sanctuary." Kenya was right and they both stood behind the door to hear the conversation on the other side of the door.

"So just think, my son Dexter, all of this is going to be yours one day to run," Mrs. Sanders told her son as they entered the sanctuary from the front door.

"You think so, Mother?" DJ asked.

"Yes, I know so. I intend to make it happen for you just like I made it happen for your father. I wouldn't trust just anybody to take over for your father when he retires. You are our son, our seed and the heir to the throne of New Life Christian Church. Listen to me. You will not marry just anybody. You will marry somebody worthy of you and worth something too. These little girls running around here aren't going to amount to much of anything but housewives, mothers, and a few may become professional nurses or teachers. I emphasize the word may loosely. I am looking for a wife for you who is your equal. Just like the President and Mrs. Obama. They are equals. They are both smart, intelligent, lawyers and in power positions. They didn't come from money like you have, but they both had the drive and will to succeed. That's what I am trying to instill in you," Mrs. Sanders insisted.

"What about love?" DJ asked.

"Love!? Love, son, is for poor people. We are not looking for love but position, power and prestige," his mother said emphatically.

"Weren't you in love with my father?" DJ inquired.

"Of course, but I knew that he was going to be somebody one day and I was going to help him to get there and keep it," Mrs. Sanders continued.

Kenya and Sierra stood still to hear all of Mrs. Sanders' lofty plans for Dexter, Jr. and the future of the New Life Christian Church. The longer they listened, the more complex and controlling her plans became.

Kenya whispered, "I told you that he wasn't worth your time and his mother ran everything. She is a snob and it would never work. You would spend all of your life trying to please her even if you got a chance with DJ."

Sierra answered, "You were right. I can hear it in her voice. What was I thinking?"

"That she was a normal person," Kenya added.

"Right," agreed Sierra. She was convinced that God could do anything. Hearing the words coming directly from Mrs. Sanders about her plans, instructions and the apparent agreement by DJ, Sierra realized that her little sister was right. She should put that dream aside and go on with her own plans for her future.

Kenya opened the door and Sierra followed, to the surprise of Mrs. Sanders. They didn't interrupt or speak at first, but Mrs. Sanders spoke first "Hello, girls, what are you all doing?"

"Our mother told us to collect the decorations here in the sanctuary because the decorator had to leave," Kenya offered.

"Oh, okay. Well, get to it," Mrs. Sanders said sharply.

Mrs. Sanders looked to see if either girl flirted, noticed or even looked DJ's way. Fortunately, both girls ignored DJ and just began to take down the decorations and only spoke to each other.

DJ wanted to speak, but his mother said, "Let's go, son, we have other things to do today." They continued toward the right side of the front stage and Mrs. Sanders went through the door first. DJ turned back to look at the two young girls taking down the decorations with light banter.

DJ thought, *I hope that one day I will be able to marry someone who will love me for me and not for who and what my parents are or what they think I will be.*

School

That day, overhearing Mrs. Sanders' words, had an immediate effect on Sierra. She graduated from high school with honors as expected and went on to apply, be accepted to and attend Ohio State University in Columbus, Ohio. She won many scholarships, grants and donations from church members who wanted to support her success. Her parents and entire family were proud of her. She was proud of herself and her accomplishments. Sierra loved music but knew she needed to be practical with her studies. She decided to major in Business, minor in Spanish because she had taken the language for four years in high school and a second minor in International Affairs. She also wanted to take some classes in Journalism. Her parents always reminded her to be as prepared as possible because, 'You just never know where your life will take you.'

Music and technology were both outlets that Sierra loved. Ms. Jillian had told them on a youth retreat that Sierra was gifted in music just like she was and she would always have that gift and it would never go to waste. Sierra sang any chance she got, but she also knew that her parents encouraged all of their children to have a marketable degree and skills to fulfill their goals of independence and success. Ms. Jillian owned a huge Information Management company called "Forrester Enterprises" and was a technology influencer.

Leaving the house in the fall to attend school her first year was scary, but with the things she had been taught at home, she was very successful. Sierra won Freshman of the Year, which was a nominated award given by her professors and then voted on by her peers. She was homesick as most freshmen are, but because her grades were so good and she got along with her roommate as well as meeting so many people from around the country, she adapted very well. She finally realized that what one person wasn't interested in, other people were. She didn't date her first year. It wasn't because she wasn't asked out to plenty of dances and other events, but she realized she was on a mission and couldn't get distracted by a relationship. She had seen countless girls go home after the first or second semester because of grades or pregnancy. Sierra was determined not to do the same thing.

Dexter was also attending Ohio State just like Sierra. He was a Business major and minored in International Studies. They only had a few classes together because of the pre-requisites of their different majors. Dexter never acknowledged her presence on campus, not a hello, nod, wave or smile. It was like those years in church youth department, camps and retreats never happened. He didn't have to ask her out but not even to speak? That was disrespectful and she understood what being invisible to a person was all about. She also remembered all that Dexter's mother had said at Ms. Jillian's wedding that day, so she ignored him right back. She watched as he dated girl after girl but stayed her distance and didn't force her way or engage him in the least. The girls on campus swooned over him, but Sierra kept her composure and focused on school instead of Dexter's looks and charm.

The Wrong Class

One day during freshman year and second semester, she was taking a music appreciation class. It was an elective, but anyone could take it no matter the major and it counted. Who walked in the room but Dexter? He was late and the only seat in the room was next to Sierra. He sat down, and like normal, he said nothing and she said nothing back. Until the professor asked, "Welcome to Music Appreciation 101. I want you to turn to the person to the right of you and introduce yourself."

Well, Dexter was on the aisle seat on the end and he was to Sierra's right so she spoke first. "Hello, I'm Sierra Campbell from Cincinnati. What's your name?"

"You know me."

"Yes, but apparently, you don't know me because you haven't acknowledged my presence this entire year, so I thought I would change that."

"Whatever, but I do know who you are."

"Great, but you haven't said your name and properly introduced yourself."

"And I'm not going to do it today, either."

"By the way, aren't you in the wrong class? I'm quite sure that Music Appreciation is not a class for the future Pastor of New Life Christian Church," Sierra said with a smirk.

"Oh wow, you came for me but I'm not in the wrong class. By the way, why can't I be in Music Appreciation 101?"

"It's a free country, but I just find it interesting."

"All right, class, does everyone know the person sitting next to them?"

Sierra raised her hand and said, "No, sir, this guy doesn't want to say his name."

"Young man, what is your name and where are you from?"

"I'm Dexter Sanders from Cincinnati."

"Now you know his name, young lady, and you, sir, that is a zero today for participation."

"Girl, are you crazy?" Dexter said under his breath.

"No, I'm not crazy. I am a human being and I will not be ignored." Sierra was satisfied that she got her point across but knew that after today, she would never be dating Dexter Sanders. He probably hated her now.

Dexter got out of his chair and moved to the front row to an empty seat just to get away from her. He thought, *my mom warned me about church girls.*

That was freshman year, and he never sat near her or spoke to her again the rest of the semester.

Sophomore year, Sierra had established a routine and knew her way around campus. This year was even more special because her sister Kenya was now a freshman. Kenya had taken advanced classes in high school and although she was two years younger than Sierra, she graduated a year ahead of everyone else in her class. They made it through the Fall Semester and it was now time to go home for the holidays.

"I can't wait to get home," Kenya said.

"Me too. I thought I was homesick last year, but I want to go home even more this year," Sierra agreed.

"Mama's good cooking and being spoiled by Dad is going to be great."

"Not to mention back in our own room and bathroom. No sharing with strangers."

"Right."

With Sierra and Kenya both in college, it was expensive, but fortunately, they were on full academic scholarship so the financial burden was much lighter. Their parents were always concerned about every bill but college was worth every dime. They wanted what was best for their children and education was always #1 in the family. There would be a couple more years before their younger brother started school so Sierra and Kenya wanted to do well in school, get out on time and get jobs to make money on their own to help out their parents. Scholarships, grants and other funds only went so far; there were still incidentals or extras.

The girls managed to get rides home with various people because their parents really couldn't afford three vehicles in the family. Two vehicles were sufficient transportation in Cincinnati, but having a car in Columbus with another payment and insurance was something that the Campbells just couldn't afford right now. Sierra and Kenya worked and bought an older car, but it wasn't safe enough for the 100 mile drive back and forth to school. So it stayed parked in Cincinnati.

The trip home this time was by bus. Mr. Campbell arrived at the bus station to pick up the girls.

"Daddy!" they both shouted just like they did when they were little.

"Hey, girls! So glad that you're home."

"We are too!"

Mr. Campbell helped them put their luggage into the car and once back on the road, they talked and laughed all of the way home. "Your mother has made all of our favorites tonight. I hope you're hungry,"

"What college student is not hungry? It's like a tape worm is put in our stomachs the moment we get onto a campus," Sierra said.

Kenya giggled.

The holidays were always a special time for all college students. For Sierra, she loved it even more because she was home and back in the room with her sister Kenya. Not to mention, her mom spoiled her with good home cooked meals.

Her father remarked on Christmas, "Well, Sierra, you are a big time sophomore, how does it feel?"

"Not much different than being a freshman. I just know my way around that huge campus and can spot a freshman lost on campus very easily," Sierra joked.

"Well, we know you looked out for one particular freshman, your sister Kenya," her father added.

"Yep, it was easy. She was tall enough to find in the crowd," Sierra replied.

"Hey, I resemble that remark. Don't hate me because I'm tall," Kenya said.

"I don't hate you. I just can't miss you," Sierra said.

The whole family laughed, including Kenya who knew that Sierra loved her and was only teasing. The family enjoyed being together and celebrated each holiday with love, warmth and a lot of laughter.

The Forced Group

After coming back to school after the holidays of Sierra's sophomore year, she was enrolled in one of her favorite classes, "Graphic Design 101." She always loved graphic design and technology in high school. College was going to be a little harder and would advance her skills, but her desire to learn more and more hadn't wavered. Because she loved it so much, she sat at the computer on the front row. There was no book for the class because everything was done online. The class was large enough for four entry doors, two on each side of the room. The instructions for logging in and to prepare for class were on the Smart Board so Sierra didn't pay any attention to anyone who came in the room.

"Good morning, class. I'm Professor Sutton and welcome to Graphic Design 101. I am look forward to all that you will create in this class.

Although you will be primarily working alone, there will be one major group project that will be required for this class. Technology is wonderful, and I love it more than anyone, but in this world, you will need to be able to work with others. We will be using Google Classroom and the assignments, videos, syllabus and everything you will need will be there. I have provided the log in and other instructions so let's begin."

Each student took the first few minutes to log in. At the fifteen minute mark, the professor said, "Go ahead and type that last sentence and let me have your attention."

All eyes were facing front. "There are two sides to the room and there are three computers at each table and four tables back. How many groups of four will there be?"

All of the students said together, "Six."

"Excellent. Now for the next five minutes, I want you to gather in your groups of four, decide on a scribe, exchange phone numbers, email addresses and decide on a date to meet either in-person or virtually. No switching seats. I have already taken a picture of who was sitting where and if you don't end up in your current group, there will be consequences."

Little did Sierra know that Dexter was the fourth person in her group when she turned around. He ducked his head but knew that he would not be able to change groups.

"Oh wow, are you in the right class?" she asked.

"Yes, smart mouth."

"Oh wow, I guess I deserved that."

"Yes, you did. You be the scribe?"

"Sierra is my name and, sure, I'll be the scribe," Sierra said and took down everyone's information.

"What's a good day to meet?" Dexter asked the other two participants while ignoring Sierra.

They each said Tuesday and he said, "Tuesday it is!"

"Fortunately, I'm available on Tuesday as well," Sierra replied.

"This is going to be a long semester," Dexter said as he rolled his eyes.

"You're telling me," Sierra added.

The others looked surprised at their banter and they all quickly sat down at their computers until class ended.

A week went past, and in this class session, they were given their assignment for the group project which would meet next week.

Dexter's friend, David, along with another boy, Justin, came in the room to meet up with Dexter to go play basketball.

"Hey, dude, did you bring your clothes to change so we can shoot some hoops?" David asked.

"Yeah, I got them. I'll change in the locker room," Dexter replied.

"Who is that hottie right there?" Justin asked.

"Some girl in class."

"Some girl? Dexter, you know better. She's one of the girls from Cincinnati who goes to Dexter's dad's church."

"Oh, a church girl. Nothing like it to break them in the right way."

"Justin, you've had enough girls on campus to fill campus not to mention the three you sent home because they are expecting."

"I don't know if any of them girls are expecting anything because of me," Justin said.

"Right."

"The little hottie taken or dating somebody?"

"I don't know, and I don't really care."

"Oh, so you saying free game?"

"I guess. Do what you want to do."

"Dexter, that's not right. Don't sic Justin the hound dog on that girl," David intervened.

"David, I don't care," Dexter said.

"Great. You gonna introduce me?"

"No way."

"Let's go play ball."

Justin eyed Sierra the whole time she was packing her backpack and she never saw him watching her.

Class met on the next Tuesday. Sierra and the entire group showed up on time, did their work and got quite a bit done toward their project.

"Well, that worked out well," Sierra said while she was packing her book bag.

"I agree," Dexter said.

"We finally agree on something."

"I guess."

"Is that a smile I see?"

"Nope, my lips just got caught above my teeth."

"Wow."

The study room opened and Justin popped in the door. "You ready?"

"For what?" Dexter asked.

"Sure," Sierra said with a smile.

They had answered Justin simultaneously and Dexter looked totally confused while turning his attention from Sierra to Justin. "Oh, man."

"Yes, man," Justin said with a huge smile.

Sierra grabbed her things and headed to the door.

"After you," Justin said while holding the door. He turned back to Dexter a gave him a wink.

Dexter said in a whisper and mouthed, 'don't do it," while waving his hand under his chin.

"My father always said that dogs chase cats," Justin said softly and then laughed as he went out the door.

Dexter rolled his eyes again while gathering up his backpack and headed back to his dorm.

It was Taco Tuesday on campus. The tacos were $.99 so there was a crowd in the student center.

Justin and Sierra walked through the line, gathered their food and then headed to a table. Justin was a smooth talker and he could make Sierra laugh, so their time together was fun. When they were finished, he walked her to her dorm building.

"So I had fun," Justin said.

"So did I."

"So are you going to ask me up to your room?"

"Why?"

"Well, I thought since we had so much fun together, we should continue having even more fun."

"Because of sitting at a table with you for an hour eating tacos? Not to mention that I paid for the meal with my own meal card? Now, you think that you have a right to come in my room that I share with a roommate, and do what?" she asked.

"Well, we could get to know each other better."

"I think I know enough."

"No, I haven't shown you my good moves yet." Justin moved in closer, in hopes of a kiss.

Sierra dropped her purse and backpack simultaneously and went into her karate stance, punching him in the stomach and then the eye. "Mr. Chin's class on Reading Road. That was my very good black belt move," she told him.

"Girl! Are you crazy?"

"No, you are! You'd better be glad I didn't drop kick you down the steps. I am here on a full scholarship. I will be going home in two years with a degree and not a baby! Boy, bye," Sierra said as she picked up her backpack and purse and went into her dorm building alone.

A few minutes later, Justin walked very slowly into his own dorm holding his eye. He walked past Dexter and David's dorm room and the door was open.

"How was Taco Tuesday?" Dexter asked. David looked up from his laptop too, to hear Justin's answer.

"Shut up!" was all that Justin could say.

Dexter chuckled slightly.

David said, "Wow, look at your eye!"

Dexter thought, *my respect for the church girl just went up.*

The next day Dexter passed Sierra in the fine arts building just as he had all semester, headed in the opposite direction in the hallway. Sierra had her ear buds in with her head down so she didn't see Dexter until he touched her on the shoulder.

"Hey, how was Taco Tuesday?" he asked.

"The tacos were great, but your friend was not."

"From what I saw, you handled yourself rather well."

"Thank you, I guess. My dad warned us about guys like him. That's why he put us all in karate class."

"Good for you. See you next Tuesday."

"See you around." Sierra put her ear buds back in and smiled all the way to class, saying to herself, *he didn't ask you out. He's got a girlfriend. He was just being nice and that's all.*

The next Tuesday, the group met for the final meeting before Christmas break. "Sierra, do we have everything we need?"

"Yes, everything is on the Project Google folder on our shared drive. I'm going to go over everything just to double check during dinner so that I can upload everything by tomorrow. That way, we can turn it in early before break," she answered.

"Great. Sounds like a plan. Anything else from anyone else?"

The rest of the group shook their heads no and packed up to leave for the evening.

Dexter was pleased with all of the progress of the group. He was a natural leader in the areas that interested him, but preaching was not one of those areas. The group would be making a virtual, formal presentation to a local company with a new logo, layout for a website upgrade, as well as social media graphics. This was a year-long project so this same group would possibly be working together in the spring.

"Sierra, where are you getting dinner?"

"I'm just grabbing some tacos to take back to my dorm," she said.

"Well, why don't I join you in the commons and go over everything with you to double check things so you won't have to do it all yourself?" he suggested.

"That's fine." Sierra could hardly breathe, but she remained calm while trying not to trip over her own two feet while they headed to the Student Union and then to the commons area to work with strong wi-fi.

They ate their tacos in silence and then Sierra opened her laptop and they began reviewing the documents in the folder based on the project checklist.

"What are you doing?" a young woman asked rather loudly, along with tapping her high-heeled boot on the linoleum floor.

"Britton, what are you doing here?"

"I came to get some food, happened to walk by and see you all cozied up with whatever her name is."

"Her name is Sierra, and we are working on a project. Did you not notice the laptops?"

"Yes, but you cancelled on me," the girl said.

"Yes, and what about it?"

"Can we go somewhere? I don't want her hearing all of our business."

"I'm not going anywhere until you stop talking and acknowledge Sierra," Dexter said.

"Okay, sorry. Sierra, is it?"

"Yes," Sierra replied.

"Sorry, Sierra."

"I'll be right back," Dexter told her as he stood.

Sierra didn't know what to do but decided to do what she thought was best and packed up her things and left.

When Dexter returned from the very heated conversation with Britton, there was a note on his laptop. *I'll finish up and share the document with you. Let me know if there is something that I missed.*

Walking back to her dorm, Sierra's emotions were all over the place. She was mad, angry, sad and excited that Dexter had at least stood up for her. On the other hand, she was having a great time with him working on the project even though she knew that he was dating someone else. Tears wouldn't come.

She passed Kenya's room and her door was open.

"Hey,"

"Hey. Sierra, you okay?"

"Yes, I'm fine, just tired, but I've got some work ahead of me tonight before I go to bed."

"Well, get it done, take a hot shower and then go to bed," her sister suggested.

"Yep, that's what I need. See you later."

"Night."

When Sierra got to her room, tears welled up in her eyes but she wiped them away quickly. She didn't have time to be sad; she had a project to finish, with or without Dexter. Her mother always said, 'in spite of your feelings, you have a job to do, finish it. We're Campbells, we do our best and finish.' She unpacked her backpack on the desk and turned on her laptop. When it finished booting, there was a Google Hangouts message.

Sorry, Dexter

You're good.

No, that was not good. I wish you had stayed and we could have finished. We only had a little left.

I got it.

Log in now, share it, and let's work on it remotely.

K

It didn't take but about twenty more minutes to finish the project. Sierra saved everything, copied everyone and turned it in to the professor early, rather than on time.

Great job, Sierra, and good night.

Thanks. Goodnight.

Sierra was satisfied that the project was completed but still concerned about the scene earlier. Trying to put it out of her head, she gathered her things and headed to the bathroom for that shower. As soon as she got in the bathroom, two girls she didn't know came in, and a third girl, one she did know, came in right after them, Britton. They locked the door and stood in front of it like some mob scene in a movie. She could have easily run for help because there were multiple doors in this common bathroom area, but her father said, 'if you start running, you'll always be running. Fight if necessary and even if you lose, you had the guts to fight instead of running scared.'

"So they tell me that you're Cincinnati Sierra."

"No, my name is Sierra and I am from Cincinnati," she replied calmly.

"Whatever. Me and my friends came to let you know that Dexter is my man and you are to leave him alone."

Sierra said nothing. She continued to fill the sink with hot water and was looking down, but she could still see out of her peripheral vision. Mr. Chin used to say ignore your opponent if possible, but if they attack you, be ready and take down the closest one to you first.

Britton came closer. "Did you hear what I said?"

"I hear very well."

"Good, now listen here…"

Britton came in even closer to Sierra's already limited personal space. Too close for Sierra. When the girl raised her fist like she was going to hit her first, Sierra took the hot washcloth and wrapped it around her arm, twisted her arm behind her back and twisted the other arm to match it. Just that fast. Britton was suddenly turned to the side and Sierra was well prepared to use her feet if necessary.

"That rag is hot! Get it off me!"

"I will, but after you listen to me. Dexter and I are in the same class and working on a year-long project. That is all. Do I make myself clear?"

"Very."

Sierra immediately released Britton and the lock on the bathroom door turned. It was Mona, the Resident Assistant, or RA, unlocking the door.

"What's going on in here?" Mona asked when she entered. From the back door, Kenya came in.

"Nothing, just having a friendly conversation," Britton said.

Sierra didn't agree or disagree. The other two with Britton were standing there not saying one word, trying to look innocent which was very hard.

"With the door locked, that's a very private conversation, which is held in your room and not in the bathroom. Secondly, rule number one in this dorm is we don't lock the outer doors, just the bathroom stall or shower stall while you're using it. A dead giveaway that something was not right. Now, ladies, since you are not residents here and apparently not a guest of someone here because you would be in their room and this door would not have been locked, I suggest that you leave immediately."

"No problem, we're leaving.

"Thank you."

"What happened, Sierra?" Kenya asked first.

"I'll tell you later after I shower," Sierra said, looking her sister straight in the eye. That's the way their parents taught them to be the most honest, by looking at someone straight or square in the eye. Both Sierra and Kenya both knew that she wasn't being completely honest, but pain does that. You protect yourself as much as possible until you can't any longer.

"I ain't going nowhere," Kenya said, just as serious.

"Lady, listen to how you sound after so much college education," Mona said, half smiling.

"I don't care. This is my sister and I will wait right here until she's done."

"That's a plan. I'm headed back to the desk. Sierra, if you want to tell me what happened later, you know I'm here for you. If you don't want to tell me what happened, I understand. Bullies are terrible and miserable people. But know this, unless they change, they live miserable lives. Good night."

"Thank you, Mona. Really, you can go, Kenya. I'll be okay."

"I'm waiting right here."

Sierra knew that Kenya would be standing right there when she came out and that's why she loved her sister so much. Grabbing her soap and washcloth, she ran to the shower stall, closed and locked the door. When the water started flowing, so did her tears.

When she exited the shower, she was almost startled when she saw Kenya.

"So you thought I would leave?"

"No, I knew you weren't going to leave. You are the best sister in the world and I'm grateful," Sierra said.

"Good."

Sierra finished her nightly routine, then they headed to her room and Kenya sat beside her just like she always did at home when something was wrong.

"So what happened?" Kenya asked.

"As far as with Dexter, nothing happened. As a matter of fact, we were having a good time. It wasn't a date but work on the business rebrand project. He said, 'why don't we go grab a bite and finish the project' and that's what we did."

"I know you were excited about it all."

"Sure, and nervous at the same time, but I know he has a girlfriend. I didn't sit close to him. We worked on our own laptops and that was it."

"So why the visit from Britton?"

"She saw us."

"Oh wow."

"She was furious. She asked to talk to him in private and he said he wouldn't until she acknowledged me. Britton half-heartedly acknowledged me and he was trying to explain everything to her, but she wasn't having it. They went out into the half and I packed up and left."

"Then she comes across campus with her two enforcers to say what?"

"That Dexter was her man and leave him alone. After I wrapped her up in my hot towel, I told her that we were working on a long term project together and that was it. The door was unlocked and you know the rest."

"So how did that make you feel?"

"Embarrassed and humiliated. You know how I've always felt about him, but really, she was going to gang up on me, for what?"

"Thank you, Mr. Chin."

"And Daddy for paying for the lessons."

"I wonder what all Dexter said?"

"To her, or to me?"

"To you."

"When I first got back to my room and opened my computer to finish on my own, he jumped in my Google Hangouts and said sorry. I said it's fine and he said no, it's not. We remotely accessed the document, finished it together and I turned it in early."

"That was good, but I still want to give him a piece of my mind."

"It's not worth it. Guys like that just see the outside of a person, a trophy and not looking at the person inside."

"Listen here, big sister, you are good enough in every area of your life and you never let no one make you feel otherwise. Hear?"

"Yes, I hear. I'm tired. You go to your room because I'm about to go to sleep right now."

"Love you. By the way, is Stacy coming back tonight?"

"Lord, no, she is with Samuel."

"Is it love or lust?"

"I don't know. I can't keep up with my roommate. My job is me."

"Exactly. Good night," Kenya said.

"Good night."

To say that sophomore year was eventful, was an understatement, but they all got an A on the project. Dexter broke up with Britton soon after that incident and a mutual respect was formed between them—and that was all. Dexter's mother won again. Sierra was fine with that for now, but Dexter still kept a close eye on Sierra from far away, very far away.

Home in Winter

It was now the end of the Fall Semester of Sierra's senior year and Kenya's junior year. There was a bad winter storm brewing and headed fast across Ohio. The weather service stated that it would be a very white Thanksgiving and probably a white Christmas too. There would be at least a foot of snow when it ended. It was November and the week before Thanksgiving. As predicted, the snow had already started and didn't show signs of stopping. With all of their exams finished and papers turned in early, Sierra and Kenya were going home on the Megabus and with the $10 dollar coupons in their hands, they stood close trying not to freeze. To their surprise, Dexter, Jr. was waiting for the bus as well, along with another boy, his friend from Chicago, David Washington, Jr. at the Southwest corner of Nationwide Blvd and High Street. David and

Dexter were best friends and they were seniors just like Sierra.

"Dexter's got a car on campus. Wonder why he didn't drive home," Sierra said.

"In this weather. Can you blame him?" her sister replied.

"No, but I thought he would be too good to ride on a bus, especially Megabus,"

"Oh Lord, I thought you were over him after all of this time."

"I am, but I'm just meddling," Sierra said.

"No, you're not. You are just as concerned as you ever were and you know it."

"I can't help it."

"Listen, one, he has not looked your way in that way. Two, he only communicated with you during the classes you took together and were forced to work together. Three, he hasn't asked you out in the three years I've been here, especially after you punched his friend in the face and nearly beat down his girlfriend, Britton, that time."

"Justin and Britton deserved that," Sierra defended herself.

"Yes, they both did and more. I'm proud of you, but Dexter didn't have to ask his mama to take you out up here at school. Right?"

"Right."

"So, it's apparent he's not interested, plus, he has yet another girlfriend," Kenya pointed out.

"You're right on all counts, but I can't help how my heart still feels. I've been out on dates with other people, but my heart still wonders and wants."

"The heart can want and feel, but if it is not received and reciprocated, it doesn't matter."

"You're still right."

"Shut up, girl, and keep moving so we don't freeze out here."

Sierra and Kenya kept their short distance away from Dexter and David while huddling together to keep warm.

"There's Sierra and Kenya," David said.

"Yep," Dexter answered.

"You not going to say nothing to them?"

"No."

"Why not?"

"Because my mother told me I couldn't and shouldn't date girls from the church and we're not in a class together right now, so I don't have to."

"Do you know how you sounded right then?"

"How?"

"Like a punk," David said.

"I'm not a punk."

"Yes, you are. First, going over to stand with two girls from school and your church does not constitute a date. Secondly, you've taken at least two or three classes with Sierra and worked with her on a year-long project. Finally, for me, her sister might be a year younger but, oh so gorgeous."

"You talk to her."

"Don't dare me."

"I just might."

"You don't have to. I can talk to her on my own, but first, listen. I love your parents, but your mother is going to control you for your whole life if you don't finally stop it."

"I know, but what do I do?"

"You be a man. Stand up for yourself. Change your major. Get the degree in what you want to get it in and love what you do. Not the degree they want for you and the life they want for you, but live your own life. I watched my mom be put down and controlled by my dad for the first five years of my life. I didn't know it at the time. I thought that's how most men were to women. I was not nice to most men who tried to date her because in my little boy mind, I was trying to protect her. I didn't want her hurt by another man until her new man, my dad, Mr. Myron. He's nothing like that. He supports and encourages my mom in everything she does. She is the happiest I've ever seen her. I want to make a woman happy like that one day and you should too."

"How did you get so smart?"

"I don't know, but I'm glad that I can be myself and be supported in my life choices instead of being controlled by someone else," David told him. Then he did just what he wanted and headed over to Sierra and Kenya.

"Y'all all right over here?" he asked.

"Yes, but freezing," Kenya said.

"The bus was supposed to be here twenty minutes ago," Sierra said through chattering teeth.

"I think I hear it coming now. Is your dad coming to pick you guys up when you get home?"

"Yes, he always does, no matter what."

"Good."

"You staying with Dexter, or are you going home to Chicago?" Kenya asked.

"We are all staying in Cincinnati this year. My mom, my dad, Myron and Aunt Jillian and Uncle Byron."

"That sounds like fun."

"Yes, I'm looking forward to it. Hopefully we can all get together before we go back to school."

"Maybe, we'll see."

"I'll try to make that happen," David said, looking directly at Kenya.

Secretly, Sierra still held a faint torch in her heart for Dexter. The other guys on campus she dated took her for a few chicken wings and movie dates but nothing serious. She had a stubborn streak. She now realized that there was nothing worse that holding out for the one guy who wasn't really interested in you and passing up guys who were actually wanting to spend time with you.

The big blue Megabus finally arrived. With the snow falling as well as the temperatures, Dexter and David were at least gentlemen and allowed them to get on the bus first. Dexter still said nothing. There were four seats left so Sierra and Kenya sat on the two seats to the right and Dexter and David were on the other two seats across the aisle from them.

The Snowstorm

The bus pulled out from the Columbus stop just like normal. The snow was still coming down, which was normal for Ohio. All Ohio natives know that in winter there will be snow; sometimes a lot or a little, but there will be snow. The bus travelled on its normal highway straight down I-71 South. It was only a hundred six miles from Columbus to Cincinnati, so within two hours, they would be seeing their parents and a happy holiday all would have. There were only a few non-students on the bus so most of the people knew each other. As they travelled south, which should have provided better visibility and less snow, it was quite the opposite. The snow was deeper and the visibility was worse. All were concerned, but as long as the driver could see, things were going to be all right. But then the dispatcher came on the speaker and said, "I-71 is now closed and you're going to have to pull off the road and seek safety."

It was quiet on the bus after that announcement.

"Seek safety?" Sierra said out loud.

"That's what the man just said," Kenya replied.

"Where?" Sierra asked.

Suddenly, the bus pulled over and the driver came on the speaker. "Okay, folks, in typical Ohio weather fashion, we're going to have to stop and hunker down at least for tonight. Hopefully, in the morning, we will be able to continue on to Cincinnati. There is a small, very clean motel that has agreed to put us up for the night at a discounted rate. I know the managers and it is at the next exit. To avoid a major cost, I suggest that you group together with four of you in a room for convenience and cost. They don't have enough rooms for only two in a room. I wish I could change the weather but I cannot, but I will get you to safety. Thank you for choosing Megabus and so sorry for the inconvenience."

David said, "Okay, it's going to be the four of us in a room," speaking directly to Dexter, Kenya and Sierra.

"Are you telling us or asking us?" Sierra asked.

"I'm telling you because it will be cheaper to split the room no matter the cost. You have another suggestion?"

"Let me talk it over with Kenya."

"Okay," David said and turned his back while the two girls whispered.

"You okay staying in the room with these guys?" Sierra asked Kenya.

"Yes, we can set the room rules. No undressing except in the bathroom and if they are okay sleeping in the same bed, so are we," Kenya said.

Sierra turned in her seat away from Kenya, back to face David. "Okay, you've got a deal. You determine how you guys are going to sleep, but we're sisters and we'll be in the same bed together."

"Don't worry, we'll work that sleeping thing out," David said.

When they arrived at the motel, the driver said, "I need you all to text me your names and a contact phone number so when the highway opens, I'll text you the time we'll be leaving. We need one person from each room to go inside, check in and text me the names and room numbers to 555-1515. Be careful exiting the bus."

David jumped up in the aisle and turned to the three of them. "I'll take care of texting the driver and, Dexter, you get the room. You guys hold on and we'll be right back." David and Dexter headed toward the front of the bus.

"I like the way David takes charge. He's not controlling but takes charge when necessary," Kenya said.

"Me too," Sierra agreed. In the back of her mind, she thought, *that's the kind of guy I'm looking for. Not just looks but will stand up for me in the situation when necessary.*

Moments later, they arrived in Room 210. "What's our part of the room, Dexter?" Sierra asked.

"That's okay, don't worry about it," Dexter said.

"Oh no, we are going to pay our share," she insisted.

"The room was $40 and with tax is $43. So you guys' half is $21.50. Hopefully, we will only stay one night," Dexter said.

"Hopefully. I want to be in my own bed and room by tomorrow," Kenya said.

"Exactly. Here you go, Dexter." Sierra handed him exactly $21.50.

"I see you got your stash, sister," Kenya teased.

"Always a stash." They both giggled.

The cable was out because of the storm but there were heat and lights and they were safe. Kenya called home, explained what happened and why they wouldn't be at the bus stop. Their parents said that they were glad they were safe.

When David called his family, they were equally glad that he was safe and sound. When Dexter called his house, he went into the hallway. He suspected that he would receive a totally different greeting than the others from his family, especially his mother.

"So, son, I'm glad that you're safe and hopefully, this storm will let up soon. Get ready because your mother wants to talk to you," his dad said.

"Give me that phone, honey. Dexter, I'm glad that you're all right but you're in the room with David and two other girls from church?"

"Yes."

"Why?"

"Because it made the room cheaper,"

"We're not poor! You could have gotten a room to yourself without David or those other two girls."

"Mom, how do you know that there are four of us in the room?"

"Because there was someone on the bus who knows you and called me."

"Really, Mom? We're in a snowstorm!"

"Don't you raise your voice to me, young man. I'm still your mother."

"Yes, Mom, but we're in a snowstorm. Sierra and Kenya go to our church and we know them. I'm not dating either one of them. We were just on the bus together in a snowstorm."

"Listen, young man, your reputation is all you've got."

"Yes, ma'am!"

"Call us as soon as you get back on that bus and I hope it is first thing tomorrow morning. I want you to be in church on Sunday and not in some hotel room with two girls who could blemish your reputation."

"Yes, ma'am."

"Good bye and I love you."

"Love you too."

Even though Dexter was in the hallway, it was hard not to hear his side of the conversation. When he came back in the room, three pairs of eyes were looking at him.

"My mom. She worries a lot," he said.

All three of them looked back down at their phones.

About twenty minutes later, "Anybody hungry? I always keep snacks. I had extra money on my meal card and filled up before we left," Kenya asked. She pulled out chips, cookies, fruit roll-ups and a couple of apples too.

"Sounds good. I saw a soda machine. I'll get some drinks," Dexter said, leaving the room. The cold air would do him good to clear his mind and get him away from the others. Embarrassment and humiliation were not his favorite scene but how he would get over it and stand up to his mother, he would never know. She always seemed to find a way to manipulate him. When Dexter came back with an array of drinks, there was a picnic arranged on the room desk and they all shared.

Back on the Road

"It's not filet mignon, but it'll do," David said.

"You got that right. How about a game of UNO?" Kenya added as she pulled out the small box of cards.

"Great idea! It's me and Kenya against Sierra and Dexter," David said with a smile.

"Prepare to get beat really good."

"I didn't know you could play in pairs?" Dexter asked.

"Too much church for the church boy."

"You got that right," Sierra said and they all laughed, including Dexter. They played about five rounds of the game and Kenya and David won three out of the five games easily.

"We won!" David yelled as he put down the last Draw 4 card on the table and put his hands in the air.

"That's what happens when you work as a team," Kenya said, putting up her hands as well.

"Yes!" David said as he high-fived Kenya.

"Whatever, it's almost 3:00 a.m., let's get some sleep," Dexter suggested.

"I agree," Sierra said.

There were extra blankets and pillows in the closet, so Dexter made a pallet on the floor and David slept in the bed since he won the last game. There was plenty of room and no problems for the very noisy and old queen-sized bed for Kenya and Sierra.

At 7:00 a.m., David's alarm with off and his phone rang immediately after. "Hello? Yes, sir. We'll be ready." After he pressed end on the phone, he told the others, "We leave at 8:30 a.m. The highway is open."

"Hallelujah!" Sierra said.

"Amen," Kenya agreed.

"You ladies go first in the bathroom."

"What are you trying to say, Dexter?"

"Nothing, just ladies go first."

"Sierra, stop trying to pick a fight and go ahead in the bathroom. You know you take a long time and I'm ready to go home," Kenya said.

"So am I."

Kenya smiled at her sister while Sierra grabbed her bag in a huff and in record time was done in the bathroom. Everyone was dressed and out the door by 8:15.

Heading toward the bus, David asked, "Sierra, do you mind if I sit next to Kenya on the way back?"

"No, I guess that would be all right if Dexter doesn't mind?"

"No, I'm fine, let's just get home," Dexter replied.

"Thank you." David smiled directly at Kenya.

There were still some snow flurries coming down even that morning, but it had let up enough for the roads to be cleared and passable. The snow was piled high on the side of the streets and the highway, but the driver drove the bus slowly and got down the seventy five miles to Cincinnati in great time and not soon enough for any of them.

Kenya and David talked all of the way home but Dexter put his coat up to the window like a pillow and slept until they got to the Cincinnati stop. Sierra closed her eyes but listened to Kenya and David. She heard the sounds of building something, maybe a relationship, but they were definitely getting to know each other. In her heart, Sierra was happy for Kenya but maybe a tiny bit jealous. She told herself, *be happy for your sister because your turn will come soon enough. Hold out. Don't settle.*

When the bus pulled into the stop, Sierra was the first one out of her seat and headed toward the door. Mr. Campbell was standing outside the car and literally ran across the street, almost falling to get to his two girls when he saw Sierra.

"You all right, Sierra?" he asked.

"Yes, Daddy, I'm fine and glad to be home."

"It's good to see you, pumpkin."

"It's good to see you too, Daddy." Sierra hugged her dad tight. She always loved it when her daddy called her pumpkin. It was his word of endearment for both of his girls. It expressed how much he loved them and was still their daddy no matter how grown up they were.

"Where's your sister?"

"She's coming."

"Oh, I see her now," he said.

"Hey, Daddy."

"Hey, pumpkin, how are you?"

"I'm fine now."

"Great, let's get your bags and head home."

"I'll get it Mr. Campbell," David offered.

"Thank you, David, correct?"

"Yes, sir."

David and Kenya were the last ones off the bus. He was also a perfect gentleman and helped Kenya with her bag while walking her to the car.

Dexter's parents were at the stop as well. His mother was still in the car but his father was waiting outside and crossed the street toward the bus.

While David grabbed Kenya's bag, Mr. Campbell walked over to Pastor Sanders on the sidewalk. "Hello, Pastor, glad our kids are home safe."

"I'm glad that you're happy about it. I just want some peace and quiet back in my house for once."

"Why, what's the matter?"

"My wife has been upset that Dexter was in the room with your two daughters overnight."

"First, Dexter was not alone with my daughters because that young man David was also there. Secondly, I spoke to them several times over the phone before they went to sleep and they assured me that they were safe and fine. Finally, Dexter is a young man. I am more concerned about my daughters safety than your son's. That's your responsibility."

"Of course, because you are their father, but my wife is always concerned about Dexter's reputation because of my position as the pastor."

"I'm always concerned about my daughters' reputation too, but this was a state of emergency, a snowstorm, couldn't be helped and definitely wasn't planned. I appreciate that your son and his friend David were helpful with my two daughters but their reputation is not the primary issue right now. Their safety is of the utmost importance, I assure you." Mr. Campbell restrained himself before he went any further. As cold as it was outside, he could still feel his collar getting a little hot.

"Maybe, but that doesn't make the environment in my home any more pleasant," the pastor said.

"Sorry to hear that," Mr. Campbell said just as Dexter walked up to his father. He realized that he should stop the conversation before any unpleasantries could be conversed.

"You got everything, Dexter?"

"Yes, sir."

"Well, we will see you all in church tomorrow."

Mr. Campbell walked away from the pastor mumbling under his breath.

Kenya was still standing outside the car. "You all right, Daddy?"

"I will be, pumpkin, hopefully, soon I will be."

"I'll see you tomorrow, Kenya," David said.

"Sure, David, tomorrow."

When Kenya finally got in the car, she asked, "What's the matter, Daddy?"

"I don't want to talk about it. Let's just go home."

"What did we do?" Sierra asked.

Mr. Campbell had not started the car but turned around in the seat to his girls. "Okay, tell me. Did either of those boys touch you two all night?"

"No, Daddy, Sierra and I were in the same bed. Dexter slept on the floor and David was in the other bed by himself. We played UNO until around three o'clock and then went to sleep."

"Daddy, that's exactly what happened," Sierra chimed in.

"Well, Dexter's mother is trying to imply something happened or it at least looked inappropriate. You can tell me the truth. I promise I'll be mad, but I'll always love you both."

"Daddy, that is the truth, we promise," both girls said.

"In four years, we're coming home with degrees and not babies. It's the Campbell way," Sierra added.

"After you're married…"

"We know, we can have twenty five kids then," Sierra and Kenya said together.

They all laughed and Mr. Campbell put the car in drive and headed home.

Scandal

The next day, the church was all abuzz. Church mothers in big hats all huddled up in threes, whispering and looking, which is never a good sign. The Campbells arrived on time for church like normal, but when they walked into the building, heads were turning, a lot of sucking teeth and plenty of side eye looks were everywhere.

"What's going on today?" Mrs. Campbell asked her husband after they found their pew to sit in.

"I don't know, but the church folks don't look very loving and inviting today. I don't know what's going on, but I don't think the 'pass the love' or the 'greet your neighbor time' this morning will be very friendly."

"I'm going to find out before church starts." Mrs. Campbell got up out of her seat and went to one of the church mothers who was not whispering and asked, "Mother Hampton, good morning!"

"Good morning, love."

"What's going on? All of this standing around in groups whispering while looking at me and my family is disturbing."

"Baby, the pastor's wife done called most of the members, upset because of your daughters being in a hotel room with her son and that Washington boy."

"What! Mother, nothing happened and it was a snowstorm, for God's, I'm mean goodness' sake," Mrs. Campbell explained.

"Baby, I know that and you know that too. You ain't heard it from me, but that woman thinks her boy is God's gift to everything. She'd better watch it 'cuz she almost half worshipping that child."

"This is ridiculous."

"I know, but remember the truth will always stand on its own and a lie will die after a while."

"I hope so because this is terrible."

"Child, the Bible said when the saints of God came together, the devil came too. He in here today. Yes, Lord, he in here today."

Meanwhile, Sierra and Kenya went to the College Service in the smaller chapel. David greeted them both at the door but smiled directly at Kenya. "Hey, what's up?"

"Hey," Kenya said with a grin, looking straight in David's face.

"Hey, David, what's up with all of the whispering and weird looks?" Sierra asked, which was the only thing that broke up Kenya and David's concentration on each other.

"I guess you guys aren't on the church gossip circle, but we are the talk of the church today."

"What about?" she asked.

"The wild weekend and possibly partaking in a lot of inappropriate behavior for college students," David explained.

"What college campus these people been on lately? There is a lot of inappropriate behavior going on!" Sierra said.

"You got that right," Kenya added.

"Well, other people can behave inappropriately but not the pastor's son," David replied.

"Oh, so that's it."

"Yes, ma'am," David replied.

"Did somebody forget to tell the gossips that it was a snowstorm and we could possibly have been in danger?" Sierra asked.

"Nope," David said simply.

"I'm going to sit down," Sierra said with disgust.

"Hey, Kenya, you free later on?"

"I could be. What did you have in mind?"

"A few of us are headed out for pizza and bowling around 6:00. You and Sierra want to come?"

"I'll ask her, but sure."

"Great, see you at 6:00."

The church services in the main sanctuary and the small chapel proceeded at normal, but Pastor Sanders made a special announcement at the end of the service. "If you are a regular, tithe paying member of this church, there will be a brief meeting immediately following service for just ten minutes."

The weekly announcements were delivered and the guests exited, then the members were asked to move closer to the front of the sanctuary. Pastor Sanders, the first lady, and Dexter were standing in front of the congregation.

The pastor began to speak. "It has come to our attention that there have been rumors spreading regarding our son, David Washington, and the two Campbell girls being stranded by the snowstorm. They sought refuge in a motel at the recommendation of the Megabus that they were on. They shared a room to save costs. There was no inappropriate behavior that transpired between the young people, I assure you. Are there any questions?"

"I have one. Did this congregation forget that there was a snowstorm and the highway was closed, they were travelling on a public mode of transportation and if there was inappropriate behavior, it is none of their business?" Mr. Campbell asked.

"I'm sorry, Brother Campbell, that you are upset, but my family has been upset by this as well."

"You are right that I am upset. I am upset that you deemed it necessary to take up the Sunday afternoon of these people to talk about being upset, but I want to know what are you upset about. Upset that there was snow? Upset that they are safe? Or upset that my daughters were in the room with your son?"

"Upset about it all. Your daughters are wonderful young women, but can you imagine how it might look?"

"More importantly, I am glad that I can look upon my daughters' faces and hug them, rather than going to look in a body bag and identify them. Let's go, Stephanie," Mr. Campbell said as he exited the pew and the sanctuary. His wife Stephanie immediately followed.

The congregation started to whisper and others left the sanctuary as well.

When the Campbells got in the car, Mr. Campbell said, "I know I was wrong but I had to say something,"

"First, you were not wrong. Secondly, I was going to say that I'm proud of the way you stood up for the girls and this family. Finally, I love you and am so glad that I'm married to you. That's all I was going to say."

"Thank you, honey. I love you too." They kissed across the front seat of the car like they used to so long ago.

The kids got in the car. "Wow, do my parents need a room?" Sierra asked.

"Maybe later," Mrs. Campbell said.

"Yuck," Sam, Jr. said.

"Go, Dad," Kenya said.

Mrs. Campbell moved closer to Mr. Campbell as he put his arm around her on the seat like they did while dating. They all chuckled and even Sam, Jr. smiled as they went home.

Dinner was delicious and they all settled down for an afternoon. Before they went to sleep, Kenya asked Sierra, "David asked if we wanted to go for pizza and bowling at 6:00. You want to go?"

"Sure, why not, I'll be a third wheel."

"First, stop saying that because David specifically asked if you wanted to go too. Two, he said a group was going so there will be more people there and I will definitely make sure you don't feel left out if they are coupled off."

"Thank you, sister. You're the best. Bowling at 6:00, it is," Sierra said as she fell off to sleep.

James

Sierra and Kenya woke up from their naps at 4:30, took quick showers, got dressed and sat waiting on David Washington to pick them up at 6:00. Promptly at 5:45, David rang the doorbell to the Campbell home.

Mr. Campbell answered the door. "Good evening, David. How are you?"

"I'm fine, sir."

"It appears the girls are ready. You all have a great time. Fortunately, the roads are clear and they also salted the hills."

"Yes, sir."

"Bye, Daddy."

Just twenty minutes later, they pulled up to Stone Lanes in Norwood. David was a constant gentleman and opened the door for both of them. Once inside, there was a group there that surprisingly were not from church but from a local young entrepreneur group in town. David introduced everyone to them and told them how he was connected and more about the organization. They all appeared to be in their mid to late twenties and no one was coupled with another person except David and Kenya, which made Sierra feel better and breathe a sigh of relief.

Once shoes were tied, bowling balls were selected and teams determined, David yelled, "Let's bowl!"

After the first game, they ate and were about to get started with game two when someone new came up to the group.

"Hey, James, glad you got here," David said.

"Hey, everybody, glad I got here too. I had some work to finish before Monday but thanks for the invite, David."

"Welcome. Join the other team; my team is full and winning. They might need some help over there."

"Hey, hey, you guys didn't win by much," someone said.

"A win is a win!"

"David, you talk so much trash."

"Well, when you're right, you're right," he teased.

"Oh, stop."

"James, right?" Sierra asked as the newcomer joined her side of the seat.

"Yes, and you are?"

"Sierra, Kenya's sister."

"Okay, nice to meet you, Sierra. I'm okay at this, but just in case I hit a few gutter balls, you'll show me the ropes?"

"I don't know about all of that, but let's see what you got."

They played two more games which they split, one each.

"James, you should have come earlier and we could have beat them three games to none," Sierra said after giving James a high five.

"I guess I should have," James answered as he held Sierra's gaze just a little bit too long.

"Uh, no, and no, James is not that good," someone said.

"David, did you see that?" Kenya asked.

"See what?"

"James looking at Sierra."

"Nope, missed it. I only had eyes for you."

"Oh, that's so sweet and thank you. I want my sister to have a good guy too."

"That's one of the reasons why I like you so much, because you genuinely care about others."

"Thank you! What's the other reason?"

"You're smart and gorgeous," he said.

"That's two reasons."

"Exactly, and there are so many more."

"I look forward to hearing them," Kenya said.

"You will, I promise."

Kenya was smiling from ear to ear.

"So, Sierra, when I came in, you guys were eating. Are the burgers any good here?" James asked.

"Yes, it was a great burger," she said.

"Well, I'm starved and had no dinner. You care to join me?"

"I'm not hungry, but I'll take something to drink. Just let me check in with my sister and see if they're ready to go yet."

Sierra walked over to Kenya who was in a very close and intimate conversation with David. "Excuse me, you two, but are you guys ready to leave now or in a few minutes?"

"We can wait a few minutes. I want to play one game of pool if you don't mind, Kenya?" David looked over at her.

"I'm good. No school, I'm great. Why?"

"James asked me to sit and talk while he orders a burger and I said I would check with you guys first."

"I told you, David," Kenya said with a grin.

"You were right. Take your time and enjoy," he told Sierra.

"Will do."

When Sierra turned around, James already had a table and had ordered his food. "What do you want to drink, Sierra?" he asked when she joined him.

"A Sprite is fine for me."

"That's all?"

"Yes, I'm full, just thirsty."

"So what's your major, Sierra?"

"Really, it's a combination of a lot of things, but my major is Business with a minor in Spanish and International Affairs, but I've taken a lot of classes in Communications, Graphic Design and Journalism. I know that I can use it all in some aspect of my career and life. Some people have said that I'm all over the place, but I don't see it like that. I want to learn as much as I can," she told him.

"Excellent. I've only been out of college five years and I learn something new every day. Don't ever let anyone tell you that you're learning too much or that it appears that you're all over the place. You're not. If you're learning, you're growing. If you're growing, you will never be stagnant."

"Thanks. So what do you do?"

"I'm the Executive Administrator for Randolph Technologies and also a Project Manager for The Forrester Group."

"Oh wow, Ms. Jillian and Mr. Byron's companies."

"Yes, you go to Jillian's church?"

"Yes, I do and have since I was little. I have admired Ms. Jillian all of my life. How are they to work with?"

"Fantastic! They work the hardest of us all. I can follow leadership like that all day long. They are also encouraging me to pursue my dreams too, which is wonderful."

"Why do you say that? I thought that most employers want you to be your best."

"Most of the time, that's not the case at all. The group tonight has gone out many times and talked about the slave mentality of companies. It is for the bottom dollar, to make the company rich and you dream poor as I like to call it. That's one reason why there is so much company turn over. The employer doesn't get down to matching the employee with the right job/title/position/duties that fit them. It's all about the money for some. For us, we are in business to make money and move toward the vision of the company, but it can't be only and ALL about the money. People matter too," he explained.

"You are teaching me, sir."

Just then Kenya walked up and asked, "You ready to go?"

"Sure."

"I'm not finished eating. I'll take you home if you don't mind waiting?" James said.

"That's fine. I'm good."

"Thanks, James, see you at home, sister." Kenya walked away with a smile, toward David.

"She not ready to go?" David asked.

"Apparently not. James said he would take her home."

"Sounds like a plan. The chariot awaits."

Back at the table, Sierra asked, "So how did you get to Forrester and Randolph? I've known them a long time, but how did you meet them?"

"I met Myron Randolph at an event in Indianapolis. I'm originally from Indianapolis. I went to Purdue and was home for the weekend and the rest is history."

"Are you an engineer? I thought Purdue was known for engineering?"

"They are, but I'm a Business, Computer Science and Information Management Major."

"Which one did you major in?

"All three. I am a triple major and just got my MBA this past summer."

"Wow, so that's the reason you weren't critical of my multiple interests," she said thoughtfully.

They continued to talk about school, life, work and leisure until the manager told them it was time to close.

"Well, I guess they are kicking us out because the lights just came on," James said.

"Exactly."

He opened the front Bowling Lane door for Sierra and led her to his beautiful Lexus SUV.

After he opened her side door first, Sierra said, "Thank you, sir. I love this car. I want to be like you when I grow up."

"You already are, you just don't have the degree and the car yet, but it's coming. I guarantee it, it's coming,"

"I hope so. That's what I'm working toward,"

"That's the most important thing, working toward and on something. What's the address?"

James quickly put it in his GPS as a saved location after she told him but asked Sierra instead of the GPS to direct him instead. When they arrived at her house, he walked her to the door.

"Well, thank you, James, for a wonderful evening. I really enjoyed myself," Sierra said.

"I enjoyed myself as well and hopefully we can get together again while you're home for Christmas break."

"I'd like that too."

"Your number, ma'am?"

"That would help," Sierra replied nervously as James opened his phone. She added her name and number and pressed save.

"Well, goodnight," James said as he still stood on the top step of the porch.

"Good night," Sierra stood watching him as he watched her.

"A gentleman doesn't leave until the lady is inside the house and not on the porch," he told her.

"Oh, I'm sorry, and thank you." Sierra was so nervous that she dropped her purse and the keys flew across the porch to James' feet.

"Here you go," he said as he picked them up.

"I'm so clumsy at times."

"It happens. No problem at all."

Still, he waited as she got her key in the lock, turned the doorknob and went inside the house. Sierra went to the window next to the door to watch him leave. She said to herself, *you were terrible, but that was a gentleman.*

James said to himself when he got in the car, *I'm going to marry her one day.*

He made an excuse to call or text Sierra every day and found some way to see her each weekend of her Christmas break. It was a movie, more bowling, a Christmas Light Festival in a neighborhood nearby, as well as church attendance on Sunday morning. It didn't matter that she was in the College Group, James felt right at home. Sierra was twenty-two, not twelve, so James was fine with her age. They had spent both weekends of Christmas break together. They promised each other that they wouldn't exchange Christmas gifts because they'd just met, but James just couldn't help himself.

"Well, it's our last weekend before you go back to school. You ready?" he asked.

"I guess, but I've had a wonderful time these two weeks with you."

"I'm glad. So I brought you to one of my favorite places to eat. Normally, I'm entertaining clients, but I thought you might like it."

"I love it, and thank you."

"You're welcome. Now I don't want you to forget me when you get back on campus. You know, the guys trying to get back with you after the break. So I bought you something."

"I thought we said we weren't getting each other gifts?"

"I said you didn't have to get me anything, but I didn't promise not to get you a gift."

"You wrong for this," she said with a smile.

"Nope, just wanting to make sure that you don't forget me."

"Forget you, sir. Never." Sierra blushed slightly as she realized that she had had the best two weeks of her life. Food, laughter, movies, entertainment, notes, text messages and, more importantly, someone's full attention.

She removed the red bow and matching paper from the small square box to the name Pandora on the top. When she opened it, there was a charm that represented each day they had been together.

"This is too much!"

"No, it's not. I wanted to do it. With each charm, remember our time together. But more importantly, know that I'm praying for you and can't wait to see you again for spring break and graduation."

"Spring break?"

"Spring break."

"The charms are beautiful and thank you very much."

"You're welcome. When do you leave?"

"Tomorrow. After the Megabus issue, my parents are taking us back and doing an overnight stay. They're leaving my brother with my grandparents."

"So, I am going to hate every moment until March."

Sierra said nothing but blushed again. *Something is bound to happen to spoil this but until then, I'm going to enjoy it*, she thought to herself.

James thought, *thank God she graduates in May. I couldn't take many more of these goodbyes.*

When they arrived at her front door, "Well, this is it," James said sadly.

"Yes, it is."

"May I have a kiss?"

"You're the first to ever ask."

"Is that a yes or a no?"

"Yes."

James leaned from his six foot three frame down to her five foot six frame and only his mouth touched hers. No hands, no embrace, no tongue, only his lips touched hers.

"Good night," he said as he walked to the edge of the porch just like all of the other times and waited until she went into the house and heard her lock the door.

"Good night," Sierra said finally because she was sure that this was the best and sweetest kiss she had ever experienced in her life.

Just like that, James knew he was in love and Sierra wondered whether this was the real thing or not. So much hurt. So much pain. So many ignored her and she had to fight for her dignity that she couldn't or wouldn't hope, just pray.

From Ignored to Observed

James made an excuse to come to campus strategically every other Friday, which was the start of the weekend, to see Sierra. Between visits, he called, texted, or they would have Facetime meetings. He respected her time and she definitely respected his. He was an executive at a very profitable company but actually liked her and wanted to spend time with her.

One day the person who had ignored Sierra all of her life finally took notice.

"So what's up with James coming up here every other weekend?" Dexter asked David.

"You finally noticed."

"Noticed what? That's what I'm asking."

"James is dating Sierra."

"Sierra Campbell?"

"The one and the same."

"Why?"

"Because he likes her."

"He's an old dude. He trolling the kindergarten, I mean college campuses, for a girl?"

"Who's hating? Mr. 'new girl' every five minutes. You got your nerve. You know she secretly liked you, but you ignored her. Remember, she was the church girl your mama told you that you couldn't date."

"I know. It's fine. I just asked. I had no intention of dating her. I was just curious."

"Oh, I see. It was fine when you knew she kind of liked you, but you know James is a real man. He comes every other weekend. Kenya tells me he calls, texts or Facetimes, every single day. She's so happy for her sister. You know I'm handling mine too. What you got, Dexter?"

"More than enough."

"That's what I thought, but why you ask about Sierra again?"

"Nothing."

"Um. See you later. I'm headed to meet Kenya,"

"See ya," Dexter said, trying to suddenly mask his curiosity.

"Hey, beautiful, how are you?" David asked.

"Doing well. How are you, sir?" Kenya asked.

"Better now. Guess who asked about your sister?"

"Who?"

"Dex."

"Dexter! Why?"

"I don't know, but I told him about himself."

"Good, because I've wanted to tell him about himself for a long time, but I was waiting until my sister got over her church boy crush. I'm sure James is helping a lot with that."

"True, true, but Dexter doesn't like to be turned down."

"What does that mean?"

"Kenya, you know when people are spoiled, they think they can do just about anything they want. Furthermore, when you've got a mother who thinks you hang the moon and stars and will parade her child in front of everyone as God's gift, it can take over somebody if they don't know how to handle it."

"Exactly, I'll let Sierra know."

A few days later, it was Tuesday and time for class. The year-long project Sierra, Dexter and the other classmates had been working on was about to come to an end. Sierra had scheduled one of the common rooms in the library like normal, for them to meet.

Sierra was the first to arrive as usual. Shortly after, Dexter came in.

"Hey, where is everyone else? Are they coming?"

"No, I told them we didn't need them. We got this, you and me," he said.

"This is a group project. There is no me and you, but everybody, the team, all of us," she reminded him.

"They already turned in their stuff to me, so we just have to put it all together."

"No, you expect me to put it all together and I'm not doing it this time. We've got three more weeks, so I think we should just table it until next week when everyone is here. We can meet online so that we get a group grade and not a Sierra grade."

"What's going on? You were okay last semester. What's wrong now?"

"Nothing's wrong. This is my last major project before graduation and others should share the work load."

"Oh, so James got you up in the clouds now."

"What does that mean?"

"You feeling yourself."

"No, I'm just not stupid Sierra any more. Why, how and who gave you the authority to make that decision for the group anyway?"

"Well, I thought we could spend some quality time together."

"Quality time? I have a man and don't you forget it. Yes, I had a crush on you long ago, but that day is over." Sierra stood up, started stacking her notes and prepared to leave.

Dexter stood up also, moved in closer and took hold of Sierra's arm to try to pull her toward him closer, to stop her from packing her things, but Sierra stood firm and, thanks to her training, didn't lose her balance.

"Get your hands off me!" she said as she jerked her arm away and pushed him back with both hands in a smooth motion.

Suddenly, the door sprang open and it was James with a dozen roses in one hand, phone in the other, and an angry look on his face. Dexter looked surprised as well and just stood there, trying to look innocent.

James came closer to Sierra and said, "Hold these while I do this." He handed Sierra the roses with his right hand and immediately punched Dexter in the face with his left. Dexter fell to the ground in pain with a bloody nose.

"If you broke my nose, I'm suing," he said.

"Sue me because I saw the whole thing through the window. Oh, you forgot about that, didn't you? You don't lay your hands on a woman who apparently doesn't want you and especially not one who's with me and whom I love."

"She used to like me like that."

"Yeah, she showed you how much she still does, which is not at all. Let's go, babe," he said, turning to Sierra.

"Gladly," she replied.

James opened the door for Sierra to exit the library.

"What are you doing here and how did you know I was in the library?" Sierra asked.

"I had a business meeting with a client in town so I called David, who was with Kenya, and she told me. I wanted to see you, surprise you and hopefully take you to dinner and not Taco Tuesday," James explained.

"This is a great surprise, and I'm so glad to see you too. The flowers are beautiful!"

"I'm glad to see you as well. Glad you like the flowers. But I didn't expect to have to punch him out like that."

"Me either. He's never done that before."

"Some guys are like that. Spoiled, demanding and feel entitled to something that they clearly don't deserve."

"Clearly. Sometimes I can hardly believe that I deserve you."

"I feel the same way but so glad that we found each other," he said with a smile.

"Let me go change because I'm starving."

They walked hand in hand to her dorm. James waited patiently while Sierra changed.

"I see that James found you," Kenya said.

"Yes, he's downstairs."

"We saw him in the lobby when David walked me back. He's talking to him now. I told James I would come up and help you so it wouldn't take so long,"

"Thanks. You know I'm slow sometimes," Sierra said with a laugh.

"That's why I came up to help."

"Aren't these flowers gorgeous?"

"Beautiful, but don't get distracted. I'll put them in water while you change."

"Thank you. You're the best. I'm rushing as fast as I can."

"Hurry, don't keep a good guy waiting,"

"Kenya, he said that he loved me."

"Did you say it back?"

"No, it wasn't the right time. He was angry at Dexter at the time."

"Yeah, we heard that James punched Dexter in the face."

"Bloody nose and on the floor. Priceless. I didn't see that one coming."

"Apparently, Dexter didn't see it, either. Hurry."

Sierra emerged downstairs in a cute pantsuit and light makeup.

"Well, I guess I'll let you two go to dinner. Don't mind me, I'm nobody," David said as he watched the exchange between James and Sierra. Kenya was around the corner, looking as well.

"David, he told her that he loved her."

"I know. He told me too."

"You know I love you too, right?"

"I do now, and I love you right back," he said.

David and Kenya kissed in the hallway of the dorm, not caring who walked by. That's what love looks like.

Neither James nor Sierra said anything, just had their eyes locked on each other.

"You look gorgeous," he finally said.

"Thank you."

"You ready?"

"Yes."

"Let's go," James said as they headed toward the door. They had a quiet dinner at a Bistro in town while trying to put the earlier incident behind them.

As he drove back to her dorm, there was smooth jazz on the radio and they still held hands while leaning on the car console.

When James parked the car, Sierra turned to him and said, "You said you loved me. Did you mean it?"

"Of course, I meant it. I was angry at the time at Dexter, but I meant every word. I probably should have said it at a different time and place but oh, I meant it."

"I've never felt or been treated like this before so this feels like a dream sometimes."

"Why?"

"You imagine something in your mind..." she tried to explain.

"That it would have been Dexter," he finished for her.

"No, not him at all, but the mere dream of how the person, whoever they are, would treat you, make you feel and want to be with you and you want to be with them. I watched Ms. Jillian and Mr. Byron on their wedding day and said, 'I want that one day,' but didn't have a clue what that would look like or be like. I don't know whether it is real love or not, but I like it and don't want it to ever stop. I love the roses and they are beautiful, but what I love most is that we have so much fun together but you really want me to succeed. You want me to be my best self. You support my dreams."

"And I always will."

"I have watched my parents and know that there are compromises in relationships, but you can't and shouldn't compromise the real you, the inner you. No one is worth that, no one."

"I agree."

"Some things must be done at the right time and in the right season. Some things have to be put on hold and other things take priority, but at the end of the day, what is your purpose and what were you born to do? Do that. Pursue that," she said.

"Wow, such wisdom. Proud of you for seeing that."

"Thank you."

"So, I have to know. Are you saying you love me back, or are you still thinking about it?"

"No, I love you, but I'm scared and happy all at the same time."

"Love is a risk but a good one, and I think being a little scared of the new situation is normal, but never be scared of me. I never want you to feel that. My mom was scared of my dad for years, and I told myself that I would never make a woman feel that way about me," James said.

"Thank you, because I haven't grown up in a house with a lot of conflict between my parents. They have disagreed or they have both been angry about one thing or another but fighting, arguing, hitting each other has never happened in our house. My parents are not perfect people, but they just don't do that and if they do, it's not around us. If they did, we would know it and see it. I just have to ask."

"Ask anything."

"Why me? I know you've dated other people, but why me?"

"I think you're smart, beautiful, have the personality and drive that I'm attracted to, but more importantly, I knew it in here." James pointed to his heart.

He got out of the car, walked around and opened the door for Sierra. They walked hand in hand back to her dorm and said good night with one of James' famous kisses. As normal, James watched Sierra from the front step until she was safely on the elevator to her dorm. He returned to his car, called Sierra and talked to her for hours until they both went to sleep.

The next day, Sierra could see Dexter's swollen lip and busted nose from across the yard. What he said to other people about his face, she didn't know or care. She avoided him and went another path to the student commons. The graphics' class group only met online for the next two weeks before spring break because they had planned to turned in the final project before the break and be free to not meet during finals. Dexter never turned on his camera during any of their sessions because his face was still healing. Sierra didn't care to see him on camera or in-person for that matter. She just wanted to go on with her life and graduate.

It was one week before spring break and Sierra's parents called her and Kenya on a three-way call.

"Hey, pumpkins, how are you all doing?" their mother asked.

"Scared."

"Nervous, why are you guys calling us?"

"Well, your father had an idea," their mom said.

"What's that?"

"I think we should all go on a family vacation over spring break," their dad said.

"Why?"

"I thought I was working spring break."

"I was too."

"No, I think we should all take off for spring break and be together as a family, along with these two young men who are pursuing my daughters very intently," he said.

"I agree with your father."

"Sam, Jr., you don't get a say."

"Yes, I do because you guys' spring break is not mine, so I have to do my homework early because my school won't be out."

"Speaks the boy genius who had a 4.0 last time I checked."

"Right."

"Anyway, Sierra and Kenya, text your father the two young men's numbers and let him make the contact, and then we will move forward from there," their mom said.

"Agreed?"

"Agreed."

"By the way, where are we going?"

"Hawaii!"

"What?"

"Yes!"

"Awesome!"

"That's a lot of money!" Sierra exclaimed.

"Sierra, you would be the practical one. Yes, it is a lot of money, but I think my nest is going to be empty soon."

"What do you mean by that?"

"I'm just praying, planning and preparing," their dad said.

"We've been planning this for a while so we have a good-sized vacation fund. We want to use it before we have to spend it on a wedding or two," their mom added.

Silence on the phone.

"You two still there?"

"Yes, ma'am."

"Just checking. I didn't hear anything."

"We didn't say anything because you two must know something Sierra and I don't, and it must be James asking Sierra because I have another year in school," Kenya said.

"No one has asked anyone anything. It's just a feeling that your mother and I have. Don't panic. Neither of you are in trouble. As a matter of fact, we are proud of you both, all three of you, actually. We don't take vacations often and realize that we need to take one now. A big vacation this spring break. Your mother and I both have asked off from work already and I am going to ask James and David myself. Is that all right with you all?"

"It's great!"

"Perfect."

"Yeah, but I still am going to have a lot of homework," their brother said.

"Hush, Sam, Jr., get the homework done and let's go have some fun."

"Sounds all right."

"All right?! Beaches. Sand. Surf. Fun. Girls? You in?"

"I'm in."

"That's what I thought."

It was the week of spring break, and Sierra's graphics' class group was to meet the Tuesday of that week for the last time because the project was finally done. They were to turn it in to their professor, the professor was to review it, then they would all make a presentation to a surprise company for their review.

At the end of the group session, Dexter said, "Don't worry, everyone. I'm going to turn in the project for the group."

The other two said fine, but Sierra knew better than to trust him.

"Dexter, don't we have to each turn in our own assignments with our reflection papers?" Sierra asked.

"Yes, but you can send it to me and I'll turn it in for you," Dexter said.

"That's okay, I'll turn in my own work," Sierra said.

"Suit yourself."

Sierra had all of the work that they had done together because it was mandatory that it all be shared in the cloud storage and the independent reflection paper would be the only work to be turned in separately.

This class was for Sierra's final grade that was required for graduation so that she would have all three minors. She had more than enough electives and credits to graduate out right, but for the minor requirement, this was it. If the group failed, everybody failed. Dexter knew that and even though his camera was off, Sierra could hear the smirk in his voice.

By Thursday, Sierra turned in everyone's work, the group work, and the other two participants' reflection because it was in the cloud, but not Dexter's because she didn't have access. She happened to be in the technology building working on something else when her professor's assistant for her graphics' class caught her in the hallway and said, "Sierra, wait up!"

"Hey, what's going on?"

"I have your group's work for the final project as well as three reflections, but Dexter didn't turn his in."

"Why not?"

"I don't know, but I don't have it,"

"Did you ask him about it?"

"No, I didn't because I knew that you guys were working on it together and I knew that you were in the same group so I thought I'd let you know."

"So this is his revenge. He's trying to get me ineligible to graduate," Sierra said.

"I don't know about that, but remember, this class is not required for his major or minor."

"What about the other two? Do they need it to graduate?"

"I don't know that because they are juniors and not ready to graduate. So they can fail and be okay, I guess."

"That's why I hate groups! He's that ruthless that he would let us all fail."

"Maybe, but if we don't have his reflection before we leave for spring break, it'll be too late."

"Spring break basically starts today, and everyone will be gone tomorrow!"

"I'm sorry. I'm just the messenger trying to help."

"Thanks."

Sierra ran to her dorm and found Kenya. "Kenya! Open up!" Sierra was banging on the door.

"Hey, what's going on?" Kenya said when she opened the door.

"Dexter hasn't turned in his reflection paper for the group project. If he doesn't turn it in, I don't graduate! All of the pieces have to be turned in, or none of us pass. I am the only one who needs this class to graduate and get my third minor."

"Wait a minute, don't you have more than enough credits to graduate?"

"Technically, yes, but I really wanted this third minor in technical graphic design to round out my 'triple threat' and make me more marketable to companies," she explained.

"I get it, but can't you talk to him?"

"Nope, I don't want to talk to him, but I texted and emailed him with no response."

"Let me check with David and see," Kenya offered.

Kenya called David and told him about the problem.

"I'll ask him. Don't worry, and tell Sierra not to worry. I'm finishing up in the lab right now and heading back to our room. I'll let you know what he says," David said.

"Thank you."

"Welcome, I'll call you later."

"Please."

'Thank you!" Sierra yelled in the background of the phone.

When David finally arrived in his dorm room, Dexter was lying on his bed with his ear buds in his ears listening to some music with an ice pack on his face.

David walked in and slapped Dexter's foot. "Hey."

"What!" Dexter sat up quickly and ice went all over his bed. "Man, what do you want? I'm trying to rest!"

"Listen, I get it, but Sierra said that you haven't turned in your reflection yet for the group project you guys were working on."

"Yeah, what about it?"

"When are you going to turn it in?"

"I'm not!"

"You're not? Why not?"

"Because I'm getting my revenge and being mean, that's why."

"Wow, Dexter, I never would have thought that you would do something like that. Sierra liked you for years and you never paid her a bit of attention. The second she moves on with her life with somebody, you make a move on her and then when she turns you down, you get revenge. Revenge for what? Revenge, why?"

"Because I want to and I can. This is one thing that I can control in my life and that my mother doesn't control or have a say so in."

"How about turning in the reflection that is on your computer probably already done and take control of your own life and stop trying to mess up Sierra's life? She doesn't deserve that and you know it."

"True, but I'm still doing it anyway."

"Wow, the truth comes out. You are a jerk after all. It's not your mother, it's you. Your mother is not on this campus at all. This is just the way you are. We are not kids any more. We are young adults about to enter the world for real. What we do and how we treat people does matter. You have no business trying to be a preacher, minister or anything else in ministry. You need to find God and quick! I need some air."

David stormed out of the room and headed toward Kenya and Sierra's dorm. They both came down to the lobby.

"What did he say?"

"He said no that he wasn't going to turn in the reflection."

"No!!"

"I'm sorry, Sierra. I did my best."

"I know that you did, and I don't blame you. You did nothing but try to help."

"Maybe you can talk to the professor."

"I'll try tomorrow, but the campus is emptying out for spring break."

"I'm sorry, but you're going to graduate?"

"Yes, thankfully, but one person is holding up my dream, my goal, and I actually did the right thing! I hate trying to do right by myself and James, who is wonderful, but revenge by a jerk is stopping me."

"Now listen, he's not stopping you, just trying to stop. Nothing will stop my big sister even if you have to get the third minor online or in the summer," Kenya said.

"You're right and I love you for it, but why me, though? Sometimes doing what's right isn't fair."

"Yeah, but you can sleep at night."

"He ain't losing no sleep over me," Sierra said.

"True, but in the end, he will pay. I promise you, he will pay."

Just then, Sierra's phone rang. "Thanks for everything, this is James on the phone."

Sierra walked out of the dorm and started walking the quad to clear her head and talk to James.

"Hey, babe, how are you?" James asked.

"Not good," she replied.

"What happened? Something has, I can hear it in your voice," he said.

Sierra explained what had happened and James, of course, was furious.

"Do I need to come up there?"

"No, you don't. You need to focus on your last day of work, packing and getting ready to enjoy a wonderful spring break with our family."

"I can't wait to go. How are you guys getting home?"

"Dad and Mom are coming to get all of us tomorrow. We should be home by noon after I talk to my professor."

"Praying for you. Thinking about you, and you know I love you."

"Love you too. Don't get off of the phone until you tell me about your day," she said.

"Compared to yours, it was a breeze. I didn't have anybody try to sabotage my work today so I guess in the words of Ice Cube, 'it was a good day.'"

"That made me smile."

"I'm glad. I hope to put a smile on your face every day."

"Thank you. So have you packed yet?"

"Not yet, but it won't take me but a really hot minute to put shorts, flip flops, t-shirts and one nice outfit in a bag, I promise you."

"Me too."

"Promise me one thing."

"What?"

"That you will relax and enjoy the trip. Don't let Dexter or anything about school ruin it. You are able to graduate and that's wonderful."

"I promise I will enjoy the trip, but not before I go to my professor and speak my piece tomorrow."

"Agree. Now, go to bed and get some rest before I get in the car and come see you."

"I would love to see you, but I'll see you tomorrow night. Agreed?"

"Will do."

"Good night, sir, and love you for everything."

"You're welcome, but I don't know what I did?"

"Just your support and talking me through it is enough," she said.

"I'll add love in there too."

"I gladly receive it and good night."

"Good night, love."

"Night."

James knew that her plans were crushed for the third degree and he hoped things would change after the conversation with the professor, but if not, he might have to call in a favor if necessary.

Sleep came slowly for Sierra, but she finally drifted off knowing that she not only had her family's support but finally a guy who had her back as well.

Dr. Sutton

The next day, Sierra arrived outside of her professor's door a full hour before office hours. She knew that he probably wouldn't be there long so she had to make it quick. Her parents were picking them up by noon and there was some last minute packing still left to do.

"Good morning, Ms. Campbell."

"Good morning, Dr. Sutton."

"Come in." Dr. Sutton unlocked his door and held it open for Sierra as he turned on the light, put down his briefcase and sat down at his desk.

Sierra sat down at the chair in front of his desk.

"My TA told me that you might want to speak with me. I am only here for this conversation, and then I leave for vacation immediately after. I assure you that I'm only here because you are a good student and I want to hear you out. Otherwise, I'd be gone already."

"Thank you, Dr. Sutton. I am here to ask you if there is another assignment that I could add to the final project since Dexter Sanders has not turned in his reflection."

"No, there really is not because you know the assignment. The syllabus was clear and the requirements were specific that all work was to be turned in or you receive a failing grade."

"I understand that, but Dexter and I had a personal encounter that has made him not want to turn in his reflection paper."

"You are on the list for graduation. I saw it myself."

"Yes, and thank you for assuring me of that because I wasn't fully sure yet, but I want to be as marketable as possible with this third minor," she explained.

"I understand your goal, have seen your hard work and appreciate it, but the requirements for a final grade are still the same. Mr. Sanders has made his choice and so must I."

"But, Dr. Sutton, I did my part and the other two did their part as well. A failing grade would bring my whole GPA down tremendously,"

"Businesses don't hire people based on grades; they hire people based on the final degree and portfolio. You'll be fine with a major and two minors rather than three minors, with the recommendations and the portfolio that you will present."

"But, Dr. Sutton—"

"Have a great spring break, Ms. Campbell," Dr. Sutton said as he stood.

Sierra knew that the discussion was over. She picked up her purse and slowly exited his office. She walked down the hallway knowing that her GPA would possibly go down to a 2.5 from the 3.8 that she had maintained for three and a half years. That would be tragic, but she would still graduate. The worst part of it all was the fact that someone she once fantasized about dating and would have loved to marry was this heartless and vindictive. What a difference three years makes. She had a decision to make. Either ruin a perfectly good week in paradise being mad, with her family, along with a wonderful guy who loves her for real and not just in word but in how he treats her, or try to put this all aside, take the lemons and make some wonderful tropical lemonade. Sierra decided to have a wonderful time and make lemonade.

Spring Break

Hawaii was as gorgeous as the family had ever seen on the documentaries. Mr. Sanders had made reservations at an all-inclusive resort on the beach in Maui. They took a one day trip to the main land to tour Pearl Harbor and its sights but spent the majority of their time on Maui island. The beach, Luaus everywhere, flowers, beautiful sunrises and sunsets were breathtaking. Sierra felt like she was living a romantic dream. She was doing her very best to not think about school but to enjoy her family and most of all, James. Fun in the sun by day, great food and cool walks on the beach by night. James was a perfect gentleman. He hadn't grown up with a family like Sierra's but was enjoying it none the less. Even as an adult, he enjoyed seeing a whole family unit together, in harmony and loving each other. It was refreshing and gave him hope for his future. He had worked hard, put himself through school, loved on his mother as much as she would like but deep down longed for this loving family for himself and planned to get it.

There were two full days left before they were leaving to go home and nobody was wanting to go. At dinner that night, Mr. Campbell tapped his spoon against his water glass to get the table's attention. "I hope that you all have had as wonderful time here as I have. This is a dream come true, for me to give this trip to my family. Thank you, James and David, for joining us and hopefully, you have had a wonderful time as well."

"My pleasure," James said.

"Awesome time, sir," David agreed.

"Great, I have one more request. If you ladies don't mind, I would like to have lunch with the gentlemen and you too, Sam, Jr.. I'm sorry, that was a terrible joke. You are my son; I am extremely proud of you and you are every bit a gentleman. It will be our last day here. I don't know about Sam, Jr.'s plans but I plan to have my own date with his mother tomorrow night if you all don't mind."

"Oh, Lord," Sierra whispered under her breath.

"Ditto," Kenya whispered back.

"Don't worry about me, Dad. I do have plans for tomorrow evening. So, parents, enjoy."

James and David each took a sip of their water. Mrs. Campbell and Sam, Jr. just smiled.

The Conversation

The next day, the ladies planned a spa day and the gentlemen gathered at a local restaurant along the water for the most important conversation of Mr. Campbell's life. He knew that this day would come, but it was here, today and now. He thought about his own father and the conversation that they had so many years ago prior to asking Stephanie to marry him. *It won't be perfect, but here we go*, he thought.

"What are you gentlemen drinking today?" the waitress asked.

"Water for me," Mr. Campbell said.

Everyone else agreed that they would start out with water.

"I'll give you gentlemen a minute to look over the menu, while I get your waters."

"Thank you. Please bring the waters, but we'll be a minute before we order if that's all right with you," Mr. Campbell said.

"That's fine, sir, just let me know."

"Thank you." When she left, he turned to the men and said, "All right, gentlemen, I know that you are wondering why we're here."

"Yes, sir," David replied.

"Yes," James said.

"I know exactly why we're here," Sam, Jr. replied.

"I know, Sam, but let me tell them the reason. I wanted Sam, Jr. here, to see and hear this conversation and make his own decisions when the time comes for him also. But back to the matter at hand. I know that you, David and James, have great interest in my daughters. I have seen how you have conducted yourself around them. I admire that greatly and appreciate it. I also know that Sierra graduates this year from college and, James, I don't know exactly your intentions, but I have a good idea."

"I intend to marry Sierra, sir," James responded.

"That's what I thought. David?"

"I intend to marry Kenya, but she has another year of school and so do I. I have applied for graduate school and I will know my status by the end of the semester. I realize that she has another year and they have offered me unofficially a full scholarship, assistantship and stipend to stay in school another year. I can't pass it up. I played football the first two years, but it was always about school for me and not sports."

"Congratulations, David," Mr. Campbell said.

"That's great, David," James said.

"Thank you."

"Mrs. Sanders and I raised our daughters and son to be strong willed, smart, educated and independent. All of us want love and affection, but we taught them how to live on their own with or without our help. I want them to be self-sufficient even after Mrs. Campbell and I are gone. I feel it is my duty as a parent."

The young men said nothing but listened at the rationale and wisdom.

"On the other hand, James, you have your hands full. Sierra is feisty, headstrong and smart. She has dated some, but she has bloomed and blossomed with self-confidence with you. Thank you for that."

"I had a father who was not supportive or loving to my mother. I want the complete opposite in my family. I always want the person I love to know that I've got her 100%," James told him.

"Perfect. Now, she's going to be looking for a job soon, so have you guys talked about that?"

"No, sir, but there are some things that are about to happen that she is not aware of that will help her with that process."

"Oh, what's that?"

"I can't say right now, but it is going to be great."

"You sure?"

"Positive, but it is confidential right now and I can't say until it is finalized," James added.

"Where is your career going?"

"I am going to eventually leave and start my own business, with the Randolph/Forrester blessing, and be a partner with them rather than an employee."

"Wow, that is wonderful. What is your goal for that venture?"

"Randolph and Forrester are transitioning to more consulting, investments and philanthropy, rather than their daily operational tasks of events, client leads, retention, HR, etcetera. They want a project management company to oversee all of that and provide all of those roles in one shop, rather than multiple employees. We've discussed it extensively, and I have my plan in place to go independent."

"That's going to be hard starting up, isn't it, and in this economic climate?" Mr. Campbell asked.

"No, sir, because they would prefer having a business partner they know and have groomed, rather than building a new relationship from scratch. My company would stand on its own, but I would be a direct referral/affiliate with Randolph/Forrester network instead of a subsidiary. They are looking at their own succession plan and retirement within the next five years. Randolph wouldn't be my only client but my first client," James added.

They continued the conversation over lunch for at least three hours, and Mr. Campbell tipped the waitress accordingly. It was male bonding, sharing and mentoring at its best. Mr. Campbell was satisfied with the conversation and pleased with the young men and felt that the future of his family was bright.

Meanwhile, in the hotel spa, Mrs. Campbell, Sierra and Kenya were enjoying all of the amenities.

"What do you think Daddy is asking them?"

"Probably, 'what are your intentions with my daughter, young man?'" Kenya said.

"I just want to have a boyfriend when I get back home. The sudden 'it's not you, it's me' speech has gotten really old."

"I'm not there. I'm here, enjoying this wonderful massage. Hush and relax. Stop worrying, Sierra. It's going to make you old before your time and give you more grey hairs."

"Is that true, Mama?"

"I don't know, but it sounded good when I said it, so shut up."

Sierra and Kenya just giggled.

Two hours later, Sierra received a text from James that said, *meet me in the lobby at 6:00.*

Kenya got a similar text from David that said, *meet me in the lobby at 7:00.*

The next text was from Mrs. Campbell to all three of her children, *Meet your parents in the lobby tomorrow at 9:00 a.m., packed and ready to go. We are on do not disturb for the rest of the night. Love you. Mom and Dad.*

All of them texted back, *yuck and enjoy.*

When Sierra came to the lobby, James was standing there with a beautiful red rose in hand and a smile. "Good evening, beautiful."

"Good evening to you too, sir."

"Right this way."

The got into a uber town car that was waiting for them and headed around the coast to an ocean side restaurant.

"Jones, and we have a reservation," he said when they arrived.

"Right this way, sir."

The hostess led them to a candlelit table with a dozen roses in the center. James held out Sierra's chair, and once he was seated across from her, he handed her the note from the roses. *For my love with all of my love, James.*

"Oh my, James, you take my breath away, and thank you. The roses are gorgeous."

"You're welcome."

Their server came to the table, told them the specials, filled their water glasses and left quickly.

"Do you like?" James asked.

"I love it all and, again, thank you. It's something out of a romantic fairytale," she said.

"I hope I am your Prince Charming."

"Most definitely."

"So, tell me your dreams," he said.

"After college or beyond?"

"Both."

"After college, I need a job that will give me experience. I want to one day own a design/media firm and build it to empire status."

"Personally?"

"I want to be married, two kids, house filled with love, support and laughter. I don't care about the house's looks, etcetera. You can pick that, just as long as it is livable and filled with love. So what are your dreams?"

"Right now, each night, my dreams are being with you."

"Wow. I think I'm too young for this conversation."

"You're over twenty-one and just the right one for this conversation," he replied.

"Why do you say that?"

"Because I believe deep down inside, you've always wanted someone to love you the way your father loves your mother. You see it in me and it scares you."

A tear dropped from Sierra eyes.

"I'm sorry, love. I didn't mean to make you cry but just spoke the truth."

"It's not a sad tear but a happy tear, sort of. It's amazing how you can read me so clearly."

"It's because I really love you, study you and want to love you like you want to be loved, for real. Not just a pick up line or way to take advantage of you even though we are in the most romantic place in the world. Why your dad thought this was a good idea, I don't know. But I promise you this, I won't be happy or satisfied until I am able to bring you back here, alone and proper."

"I agree."

"Back to the second part of my dream. I dream of sad and hard days but having someone to be transparent with and talk out the trouble until I have a solution. I dream of having my own business just like the Randolphs, so I can be my own boss but still make it home for dinner and put the babies to bed. I dream of growing old and watching the babies grow and imparting into them what I never got from my father. I see us."

"Speechless."

"No words are necessary."

There appeared on the table a small blue box.

"Don't panic. This isn't what you think it is. This is just the promise ring. The engagement ring will come later. I want you to only think about us when I ask you. I don't want you to be worried about school, a job, moving back home, where you're going to live, just us. So this is a clear demonstration of what is yet to come. Open it please," he said.

Sierra opened the box and inside was a beautiful pearl ring with three diamonds on each side.

"It's beautiful, and thank you. It fits perfectly. How did you know?"

"Kenya," they both said simultaneously and laughed.

"I don't think I will ever take it off," Sierra said as she held her hand up to see it better in the dim candlelight.

"You will. Please leave it at home and don't take it with you back to school. Jealousy and envy are real, but our love will conquer it all. People may be jealous of us now, but they ain't seen nothing yet," he said.

"Listen at your English, sir," she teased.

"That's my Mississippi grandmother coming out in me."

"I love it."

"I love you."

"I love you more."

"Graduation can't come soon enough for me," he said.

"Me either," she agreed.

They finished their meal, returned to the hotel, and took a walk on the beach hand in hand in the moonlight. When Sierra went to sleep that night, she knew it had to be a dream until she pulled back the curtain just a little, looked at her left hand in the moonlight so she didn't disturb Kenya, and knew that it was real.

The next day, they met in the lobby for the long trip back home.

"Congratulations, Sierra. Dad told me about the ring. Super happy for you," Mrs. Campbell whispered as she gave her a tight hug.

"Thanks, Mom. I'm nervous, scared and excited all at the same time."

"That is so normal, but more importantly, enjoy it all. By the way, James is a keeper. He actually asked Dad first before he gave you the ring."

"I didn't know that," Sierra said.

"I know you didn't, but I want you to realize what kind of young man loves you. Don't ever take that kind of love and respect for granted. It is simply priceless."

"I won't, but I'm overwhelmed too."

"Being infatuated by the spoiled Dexter boy and everything that happened this semester. Kenya told me," her mother said.

"Snitch."

"No, she's not a snitch as much as she is a sister who loves her big sister and wants what's best for her."

"I know, but that was so hard, Mom. After all of this time, and then he came for me."

"When you didn't send for him."

"Listen at you, Mom," Sierra said with a giggle.

"I keep up."

They both laughed then. "By the way, Mom, where are you guys' bags?" Sierra asked.

"In the room," Mrs. Campbell replied with a smile.

"In the room? The car will be here any minute," Sierra said.

"What's up?" Sam, Jr. asked, also looking confused.

"We are not going home with you guys. We're staying another week. We just decided and booked it. Enjoy the ride back home and we'll see you in another week," Mr. Campbell said.

"Wow, the house to myself," Sam, Jr. said.

"You forgot about cameras in the house, young man."

"Just teasing."

"Love it," Kenya said.

"I'm jealous but happy too," Sierra said.

"James and David, thanks for taking care of our babies," Mrs. Campbell said with a huge smile.

"Thank you for everything, Mr. and Mrs. Campbell," James said.

"Thank you, sir," David said.

"It was our pleasure, bye to you all," Mr. Campbell said.

So the parents got to stay and play another week while the five of them endured changing planes, layovers, airport snacks, exhaustion and jet lag. They finally made it home safely. James and David said their goodbyes until the next day, then went home to unpack and rest because the next day they would be headed to Columbus for the last semester.

The next morning before getting dressed, Sierra put the beautiful ring back in the blue box. Her hand looked naked so she put her class ring on her left hand instead.

Kenya had just come out of their shared bathroom. "By the way, James said to give you this."

"What now?"

"Stop, you deserve it so enjoy."

"Okay." Sierra took a deep breath to calm herself down. She opened the card and it read, *Good morning, love. I wanted you to have something from me on your heart and hand with you at all times. James* It was a simple silver ring and matching double circled silver necklace set.

"It's another gift," Kenya said.

"I know. He is too much sometimes."

"Enjoy it. I am in love with David, and you have James."

"I know. You said it out loud and I am so happy for you."

"This is our last semester together..."

"Yes, but it's not your last times together. Remember, David loves you too."

"I know, and I am happy for me too," Kenya said with a smile.

"We've got to get dressed. We only have an hour," Sierra reminded her.

"*You* only have an hour with your slow poke dressing self. Get in the shower."

Suddenly, there was a notification on Sierra's phone. "That must be James."

"Probably wanting to make sure that I gave you the gift."

"Probably. No, it's from Professor Sutton's assistant," Sierra said in surprise.

"What does he want now? He already told you that he failed you for the project."

"I know, but he wants us to meet him on Monday morning in his office."

"Maybe he changed his mind," Kenya said hopefully.

"I doubt it, but I'm supposed to be there at 10:00 sharp. Oh well, I'll know when I get there."

"Yep, now get in the shower."

"I'm going, I'm going."

Spring Semester a Senior

Right at noon, James and David arrived at the house, packed up the truck and they headed for Columbus back to school. It was a relatively uneventful ride until it was time for James to go home. Sierra's tears flowed but James promised to call her on the way home. She didn't want him to go, but the Hawaii trip, this trip, and driving alone would be too much for him to stay too late. So with kisses, hugs and those three words that still made her blush, "I love you," she waved goodbye to him.

Monday morning, Sierra arrived at Dr. Sutton's office at 9:45.

"Right on time I see, Ms. Campbell," Dr. Sutton said as he came down the hall with his office keys in his hand at 9:50.

At 9:55, Janice and Steven from her group arrived as well. They each said hello with looks of confusion, then they all sat down in three chairs in front of Dr. Sutton's desk.

"As you all know, the requirements for the course are for all four participants to turn in all of the parts of the assignment to receive a passing grade, but Dexter Sanders has chosen to not participate and complete the assignment. I have had my assistant reach out to him many times and he has not complied with my request. He had until 9:00 a.m. this morning and I have not received anything in my or my assistant's inbox. Thus, he has received a failing grade for the project as you all have as well, which will be included in your final cumulative grade. On the other hand, I have reviewed the project and I want you to make a blind presentation to three companies that are interested in and need your type of services in their company. Sierra, you are slated to graduate at the end of the semester and if a company selects you, you may be offered a position at one of these companies upon graduation. Janice and Steven, you'll be available for internships this summer as well based on your presentation. These presentations will be blind, via ZOOM and your names are not to be on the presentation, just Group One. Your voices can be heard on the presentation but no cameras should be on. These presentations and the results are to be based on the data, systems, graphics, etcetera, and not on you at all. Understood?"

"Yes," they all said.

"Also, if you're able to sell the companies on your idea, it will be counted as extra credit toward your final cumulative grade."

"Thank you, Dr. Sutton, but what about Dexter?"

"That is no concern of yours, Ms. Campbell. I'll take care of that matter. You three have one week to prepare. Be ready next Monday at 10:00 a.m. in the Lab. Any questions?"

"Yes, I have several," Sierra said.

"I knew that you would, Ms. Campbell."

Sierra asked her questions, which prompted concerns from Janice and Steven.

When Sierra, Janice and Steven walked out of Dr. Sutton's office, they were stunned, literally stunned. The next week's work was critical. They decided to work virtually as to not cause conflict or a scene with Dexter on campus. The presentation would be virtual as well so they needed the practice. When Sierra got back to her room, she called her parents and texted James, asking him to call her later. She told him she had news. Sierra's parents were thrilled that things had worked out for her. They were disappointed about the Dexter situation but told her not to worry and to focus on what she could control, which was herself and her work.

James called later. "Hey, beautiful, how are you?"

"Better now, but wish I was still in Maui with you."

"Hopefully one day soon, but what's up?"

Sierra told James about all that had happened that day.

"I told you! Yes! I am so happy that things worked out for you."

"Thank you, love. I am relieved as well. Now for the presentation..."

"You'll nail it. I'm sure of it."

"I hope so, but we're going to be practicing every night online so we aren't bothered by Dexter."

"Sounds like a plan," James said as he heard Sierra yawn. "You're sleepy."

"No, I'm good."

"No, you're not good. The jet lag has finally set in. Get some rest and we'll talk tomorrow."

"Okay, good night."

"Love you."

"Love you more."

By Thursday, the Sanders family received a rather disturbing letter. Even though Dexter was over the age of twenty-one, it was custom that if a student applied for graduation and it was denied, an email would go to the student automatically but also a letter would go to their home residence as permanent record. Dexter had received the email already but hadn't expected a visit in the middle of the week.

There was a knock on the door.

"Come in," Dexter yelled.

There was a second knock on the door. "Just come in already," Dexter yelled again as he turned the knob on the door and opened it to find his parents standing and frowning in the hallway.

"I'm sorry. I didn't know you were here," he said.

"I know that you didn't know because we meant for it be a surprise, just like this surprise failure letter we received in the mail yesterday," Mrs. Sanders said angrily.

"I was going to tell you this weekend."

"This weekend! How could you leave something as important as this for the weekend? We have had plans, wanted to purchase invitations and invite our friends! What do we say now, Dexter? Our son failed a class and won't graduate until summer or God forbid December? Not to mention that it was some elective class of graphic design. How will that help you with running the ministry?" Mrs. Sanders said between grinding teeth. His father said nothing.

"I don't intend to run the ministry."

"What do you mean you don't intend the run the ministry? Our plan was for you to get a degree in Business, go to seminary at United, then be the youth pastor and take over when your dad retires in five years!"

"Mother, I am not called or worthy to be over anybody's ministry."

"I think I'm about to faint."

"Sit down, dear," her husband said.

"Where, in this filth?"

"Dear, it's just a dorm not an outhouse."

"Well, it smells like one."

"Son, I guess we need to have a lot more to discussions," the pastor said.

"No, sir, we don't. I failed the class on purpose."

"You what!? I think I will sit down, dirt or no dirt," Mrs. Sanders said while holding her head.

"Why, son?"

"I was angry at Sierra because her boyfriend hit me after I made a pass at her," Dexter explained.

"You did what? I can't stand anymore."

"Shut up, Marjorie. Did you press charges, son?"

"No, because I was wrong and he was right."

"Go on."

"I wanted revenge and got it."

"No, you didn't get revenge on anyone but yourself. You messed up your senior year by being a baby and not an adult. You did what kids do and not what adults do. I have told your mother time and time again that we have babied you, carried you and spoiled you rotten. This incident right here has proven it. You are officially cut off. No more allowance, no more paid tuition and no more credit card. You will come home and work for all of it yourself. I'm done. Let's go, Marjorie."

"Don't worry, honey, I'll fix it," his mother said.

"You're not fixing anything. Mess with me and I'll cut up your credit cards too."

"I'm sorry, Dexter, but you're on your own," Mrs. Sanders said as she ran behind her husband.

"Mother!"

Mrs. Sanders turned quickly and said, "Mother nothing, you messed up big time and I'm not risking my fun for you this time. Bye."

Dexter stood there dumbfounded. How would he live? Where would he live? How would he get money to do live? At twenty-three, he hadn't taken into account any of those things. He finally realized how big of a mistake that he had made trying to get revenge on Sierra. The joke was on him. He would have to fix it.

For Sierra, the week flew by. Just like planned, Sierra and her group met every day, reviewed every slide, prompt, word and format critically. As Sierra's grandmother used to say, 'no stone unturned.'

On Monday, at 9:00, Sierra texted James, *Here we go.* She was walking across campus to the lab.

James texted back, *You got this. You've done the work, now go kill it. I love you.*

Sierra replied, *Thank you and I love you more.*

At 9:30, they all were assembled, dressed professionally and the technology was up and ready to go.

Dr. Sutton was in the room with them with two iPads and his assistant. At exactly 10:00 a.m., Dr. Sutton introduced them.

"Good morning, everyone. I'm Dr. Sutton. Please indicate in the chat that you can hear me and them. Great. This is the only presentation for the marketing, promotion and rebranding of your organizations. The students only know the type of organization and the services that your organizations provide. They don't know your names, the organization's name, or any background history of your organizations. Their job is to develop a 21st Century brand strategy for information technology management service organizations. Begin."

Just like that. Sierra and her group nailed it. There was time for questions at the end via chat and it was done.

"Thank you each for your time. I look forward to hearing from you all very soon. Have a great rest of the day," Dr. Sutton said to the iPad.

"Yes!" the group screamed when Dr. Sutton gave them the signal that the call had ended.

"Excellent job from all of you!" he praised them.

"So what's next, Dr. Sutton?" Sierra asked.

"We wait."

"I hate waiting," Sierra said.

"Well, that's life and business, Ms. Campbell. Go enjoy the rest of your day and week. There are only six more weeks until school ends, so finish strong."

"Thank you, sir."

As soon as Sierra left the lab, she texted James, *We did it!*

Awesome. Let's do lunch, he replied.

Great. Just log in when you're ready. Normally, they ate lunch together over the phone or Facetime several times a week when possible.

Nope. I'm here in Columbus.

Right now?

Yes, right now. I'm in a meeting which is about to end, but I'm headed to campus to take you out.

OMG! Yes!

After Sierra pressed send, not looking where she was going, she bumped into someone.

Without looking up, she said, "Excuse me, I'm sorry."

"Yes, you are sorry," the voice said and then Sierra actually glanced up.

"Dexter? What is that supposed to mean?"

"You heard me. I said it and I'm not taking it back."

"How do you figure?"

"Are you trying to ruin my life, or what?"

"Ruin your life? No, you're trying to ruin mine by not turning in your reflection paper. David asked you. Dr. Sutton and his assistant asked you. Why, Dexter?"

"I don't know. Revenge, I guess,"

"Revenge on whom? You were willing to sabotage the whole group, for what?"

"I don't know. I was angry and thought it was a good idea. Now I'm not so sure.

"Even after Dr. Sutton reached out to you again, you still thought it was a good idea, but now you're not so sure? You need help."

"That's what David said."

"You can't keep blaming other people for your actions. The little kid song we sang in children's church, *It's me, it's me,* it's you, Dexter Sanders."

"It's amazing how I can pull any girl on this campus and you included, but you actually turned me down. The only one."

"So that's what this is about? Just remember you ignored me at church, school and when we were in the same class, but it was interesting when you thought I was someone to date or at least try something with after I was dating James."

"I guess, but a boy wants what a boy wants."

"You said it. You are a boy and definitely not a man. Boys only think about the present, but a real man has actions that can determine his future." Sierra turned to walk away.

Dexter reached out his hand. "Wait, Sierra."

"Don't you ever try to touch me or come near me again! I should press charges, but I won't. You're not worth it. For the last time, leave me alone and get some help!" Sierra said angrily.

Dexter put up both hands in surrender.

Sierra walked away to cool off so that none of that conversation would carry over into her celebration with James.

An hour later, they were celebrating over a very nice lunch, then headed to a matinee movie, bowling and late dinner. It was a fantastic day all around.

The Last Six Weeks

The next six weeks went by quickly. James was working on his plan of action and Sierra was finishing up her final college days, preparing for final exams and graduation. It was a lot of work but she was ready for it. Each week, she took a box filled with memories or clothing home to make the move out of her dorm room so much easier. It worked out perfectly since James strategically had business meetings on Fridays in Columbus and could drive her back home on the weekends, and some Fridays, David and Kenya joined them. Sierra loved it.

James was always a gentleman and texted her each morning and night before she went to bed. He didn't talk to her much the week of exams because he wanted to give her plenty of time to study. He had a box of snacks, fruit and reminders delivered twice that week just to let her know that he was always thinking of her. The other girls in the dorm were jealous, but Sierra just smiled and shared everything in the box with her sister.

The week after exams, Sierra waited for the results, worked on her resume and prepared for graduation. She received an email with a ZOOM link from Dr. Sutton for her group to meet him online that Wednesday at 10:00 a.m..

Wednesday morning arrived, and Sierra was nervous to say the least as to what Dr. Sutton would say. When she logged in, her other two group members were there, along with Dr. Sutton and an unnamed log in as well.

"Good morning, everyone. I trust that the students are enjoying the week after exams, resting and recovering from the school. I know that you are all wondering who is the fifth unnamed person on the call with us, but let me introduce to you the Executives from

Forrester/Randolph Enterprises, Mr. and Mrs. Randolph."

The camera came on and Jillian and Byron Randolph appeared on the screen. Sierra covered her face and burst into tears immediately. No noise, no outburst, just fresh, hot, tired tears.

"Hey, beautiful Sierra. Don't cry. We haven't even said anything yet," Jillian said with a slight chuckle.

"I'm sorry. I'm just overwhelmed that you're on the screen speaking to me right now. You have been my inspiration and role model, besides my mom, practically my whole life. I thank you and I don't even know what you're about to say but know that I thank you."

"Oh wow, now you're going to make me cry," Jillian said as she wiped her eyes, and the entire group smiled.

"Well, first off, congratulations to you all as well as Dr. Sutton. You have done an excellent job. My wife and I are pleased to tell you all that the presentation, the ideas, were exactly what our firm needed and we want to offer a permanent position to Sierra Campbell and two summer internships to the Janice Allen and Steven Hancock. I realize that Janice and Steven do not live in Cincinnati but these internships are virtual so no need to worry about relocating. We have plenty for you both to do in the virtual world. We look forward to meeting with you all in the future and definitely working with Sierra here in Cincinnati if she so chooses to work with us. Honey, any words?" Byron Randolph said.

"I believe that you've said it all, but know that I am extremely proud of each of you and what you presented was excellent. Let's go to work!" Jillian Randolph said.

"I will provide the contact information to each of you and how you should respond to the Randolphs by next Monday. Thank you again to you both and I hope that they are excited, as I am pleased with their work. Sierra, Janice and Steven, stay on the line and say goodbye to Mr. and Mrs. Randolph," Dr. Sutton said.

Sierra was still stunned and just looked at the screen with a slight wave, still in disbelief.

"Goodbye," Jillian and Byron said and then signed off the call.

When they disappeared from the screen, Sierra just cried and screamed.

"You okay, Sierra?" Janice asked.

"No! I am not okay but so happy that I just have to scream! I can't wait to tell my parents and my boyfriend."

"Well, I am pleased at the group's hard work but, Steven, you have said nothing."

"I am just speechless," Steven replied.

"That's a good answer but know that the internships are paid positions as well as Sierra's permanent position."

"Thank you so much, Dr. Sutton," they all said.

"You all are quite welcome. There is more to come and I suspect that the sky is the limit for you all. Have a great summer and, Ms. Campbell, have a great life."

"Thank you!" Sierra said.

Sierra texted her parents first with the details and then texted James that she had news.

James texted back, *Dinner at 6:00. Leaving work early.*

Sierra texted back, *You sure? I can't wait.*

James said, *I am sure, and I can't wait, either.*

The Campbell family was ecstatic at the news that their daughter had been offered a job with Forrester/Randolph Enterprises.

At 6:00 on the nose, James arrived with a dozen roses in his hand.

"Hey, James, Sierra will be right out," Mrs. Campbell said.

"Thank you, Mrs. Campbell."

"Hello, James."

"Hello, Mr. Campbell."

"You here for the celebration?"

"Yes, sir."

"You were right. It would all work out."

"Yes, sir."

"What would all work out?" Sierra asked.

"You getting the job and everything. We'll talk about it at dinner," James told her.

"Did you know they were going to offer me the job?"

"Yes, but I couldn't tell you because it was confidential within the company that we couldn't tell anyone and especially the applicants."

"So I didn't get the job on my own, or did I?"

"Oh, Sierra, you got the job solely on your own." James' heart was beating so fast that he thought he would faint. He didn't want to do anything that would hurt Sierra in any way and right now his hopes were wilting and so were the flowers he was holding.

"Sierra, I think you need to hear James out first before you jump to conclusions," Mrs. Campbell said.

"But I want to make sure that I got the job on my merit and not his referral. I have worked extremely hard, and I don't want anyone to just give me something that I didn't work for."

"Sierra, you worked extremely hard and deserved the position. I assure you that the Randolphs would not have offered you the job or the others the internships if they weren't convinced that you were the best for the positions. I was not on the ZOOM call when you made the presentation. I was in Columbus at the time. Don't you trust me?"

"I do, but I just want to make sure."

"Be sure of it."

"Hold on, James. Since Sierra hasn't said it, thank you for the flowers." Mrs. Campbell took the bouquet from James' hands.

"You're welcome, Sierra and Mrs. Campbell." James was confused and disoriented to say the least.

"Sierra, let's put those flowers in water. Come with me," Mrs. Campbell said.

Sierra followed her mother into the kitchen.

"Son, I told you we raised our girls to be independent and Sierra is a handful by herself. She wants to earn, deserve and be respected for everything that she gets. I apologize if this puts you in a bad position," Mr. Campbell said.

"It does, but I'll try to explain it to her later."

Meanwhile, in the kitchen, Mrs. Campbell addressed Sierra. "Sierra, young lady, are you out of your mind? What, exactly, are you accusing James of doing?"

"Putting in a good word for me and being chosen for the job based on what he said."

"He said he didn't do it, but what if he did? Do you know how many people have had to be referred to get a job, any job, in this city? You sound ungrateful and unthankful for an opportunity that others would kills to get. Did you accuse your professor of referring you to the Randolphs?"

"No."

"So why are you so quick to accuse James?"

"I don't know, but I would just feel awkward working at a place that gave me the job because I was his girlfriend."

"Well, I am going to tell how you're going to feel awkward, young lady. You are going to walk your ungrateful self-back into that living room and apologize for not being more thankful for these beautiful flowers and appreciate him for even wanting to take your stubborn self to dinner on a weeknight that he had to get off early for, drive through horrible Cincinnati traffic to come and take you to probably a very expensive dinner somewhere on his own dime! My blood pressure is about to go through the roof. You spent your time liking that Dexter brat for years, and now a very, very nice and respectful young man comes along who says that he didn't recommend you for a job, but you get an attitude and deep down, you're upset about it! I can't get you young people today! You want help and then mad when you get it. You want love from the wrong person and when the right person comes, you send them around and around when they try to love you."

"I'm sorry, Mama, that sounds terrible when you say it, but I was just thinking."

"That's your problem; you're too busy thinking about yourself. You'd better think long and hard about whether you're really ready to marry such a great young man who is in that living room or not. He's given you a promise ring that I would have killed to have had, but your daddy couldn't afford more than a thin gold, 10 carats at that, back then. You're smart in books but not very smart with relationships. Being ungrateful is not right or fair to him and definitely embarrassing to me. I thought I raised you better than that. Your brain might land you a good job, but your independence might land you alone without love. Now think about that. I'm gone to bed. Put those beautiful flowers in some water yourself!"

Sierra hadn't seen her mom that mad in years and especially at her. Had she been ungrateful to James? She hadn't thanked him for the flowers which were gorgeous. As she filled the vase with water, she knew that she had a lot of apologizing to do. What was she thinking? Of herself. Mom was right.

The kitchen door swung open and her dad walked in. "You all right, Sierra?"

"No, Daddy, I'm not all right. I'm terrible. That's what I am. Mama just gave me a good talking to and I've got to fix it."

"I agree with your mom. He's a great guy and loves you dearly. There is a young man in that living room petrified that you feel like he has tried to hurt you in some way. You and I know that even if he referred you, he did it to help you. Now, he didn't refer you and you still don't believe him. Love is so important, but trust and belief in someone is so hard to rebuild once it has been violated or even doubted. Guys don't do good with doubt. We doubt ourselves enough.

You've got some work to do to repair this. My final question to you is do you think you can live life without him? Answer that before you go in that living room," her dad said and quickly left the room.

Sierra looked at her father with disbelief but knew that he was telling her the truth. She stood there looking at the flowers. She looked at the ring on her finger and then at the kitchen door. She closed her eyes and thought back on all of the past five months with James.

James heard the kitchen door swing open. He jumped up. "Sierra, let me explain."

"James, don't say anything else. I need to first apologize to you."

"What for?"

"For everything. I am so sorry, because you have done nothing but love me, support me and promise me the world. I have worked so hard to get my degrees so that I can be independent and do things on my own that I've forgotten to acknowledge and appreciate the person who is helping me be all that I can be. Besides my parents, brother and sister, I have never been able to count on anyone else but myself. It is true but not an excuse. I want you to accept my apology, know that I love you, the flowers are beautiful and thank you. Finally, I will with everything in me strive to love you in return and live up to the life that you are striving to give me."

"I accept your apology. Now I can finally breath. I've been holding my breath for what seemed like hours."

"I'm sorry."

"I know, but are you ready to hear me out?"

"Yes."

"Come and sit down next to me," he said and then started to explain. "I knew that you were in the strong running for the position, but I was not on the ZOOM or in the room with your call with Forrester. Secondly, I am going to leave Randolph/Forrester because I want you to be there by yourself, to grow and flourish without any misunderstanding or direct influence in the same company. I love you for real, Sierra Campbell, and want to give you the wings to fly as high as you want but still stay grounded enough for us to love one another to the fullest."

"I want that too, but are you sure that you really want to leave Randolph/Forrester?"

"I have to. I have established Jones Enterprises and besides wanting to see you, I was in Columbus to make connections with other companies to get Jones Enterprises off to a great start and not just a good start with Randolph. They have been good to me and I've been good to them, but it is now time for me to be good to myself and eventually, it will be great for us."

"Wow, that's a lot to take in."

"Yes, love. Are you ready?"

"Ready as I'll ever be, but as long as you love me, keep me grounded and I strive to keep myself sane, we'll be fine."

"Exactly. Are you as hungry as I am?"

"Starving, and I love you."

"I love you more. Let's go."

The next several weeks were a whirlwind for Sierra. There was graduation in Columbus with both families, visits to Randolph/Forrester for a formal offer and to establish a start work date, all while creating graphics for Jones Enterprises, LLC, and then the ultimate happened.

Sierra began working at Randolph/Forrester on July 1st and James transitioned out of the company on August 1st. It was great seeing him every day but his time was up and it was time for a celebration. So James called a family dinner with his mother and Sierra's family. But Sierra wasn't expecting David and his entire family to come as well, which included Jillian, Byron, Vernice and Myron Randolph. Montgomery Inn was a great family spot, and along the river in the evening, was always a beautiful and romantic setting to say the least. They were all seated in a private dining area on the second floor, dinner was served and soft music was playing in the background. After dessert, James asked Sierra to meet him on the dance floor. Sierra was dressed formally by her sister and mother. James looked incredibly handsome in a beautiful navy blue suit.

"Sierra, I have waited for this day for a long time. I prayed and asked God to send me the right person for me and my life. He sent me to you after I reluctantly agreed to come bowling back in December. I am so glad that I did. I have started my company which, thanks to the Randolphs and others, is going extremely well. I am now ready to take the next step, which is..." James got down on one knee.

"Oh my goodness, my boy is about to do it. I've got to get this one on video!" David said.

"Yes," Kenya said while wiping away tears. She wasn't the only one. There wasn't a dry eye in the room.

"Will you marry me?" James asked with a 4 carat diamond ring perched high in that famous blue box.

"Yes!"

James took the ring out of the box and placed it on Sierra's finger.

"I love you," he said as he stood, embraced her and they kissed.

"I love you more," Sierra said as she fully realized that the next chapter in her life was about to begin. First, finishing college, a promise ring, a degree, a job and now engaged to be married. All in one year.

"Wow, Sierra pumpkin, what a year!" Mr. Campbell said through his own tears.

"Yes, Daddy, what a year!" Sierra agreed, wiping her own eyes filled with very happy tears.

Everyone clapped and said congratulations to the happy couple while taking pictures with their phones. It was a great night. Mrs. Campbell and Mrs. Jones said to each other, "Let the wedding planning begin!"

He Granted Her Request

Exactly ten months later, Mr. Campbell was walking his oldest daughter down the aisle to the very dashing Mr. James Jones, who was now the CEO of Jones Enterprises. Sierra was officially an employee of Randolph Enterprises and was given two weeks off with pay for her honeymoon although she had been with the company less than a year. After the music, the vows, the long, intense celebratory, "You may now kiss the bride," and the reception, the now Mr. and Mrs. James Jones were getting into the limo to begin their life together.

Just like some years earlier, this time, Kenya and David stood on the steps and waved goodbye.

"I'm so happy for my sister," Kenya said.

"Don't worry, in about two years, that will be you," David said with a big smile.

"Maybe," Kenya said, teasing him.

"Oh no, there's no maybe to it. I look forward to asking you to be Mrs. David Washington," he said assuredly.

"We'll see," Kenya insisted.

"I got your we'll see," David replied.

They both laughed as they walked up the steps back into the church.

"Yep, we shall see," Dexter said under his breath while watching close by.

About the Author

Speaker – Coach – Publisher

Julia Royston spends her days doing what she loves, writing, publishing, speaking about her why and motto, "Helping You Get Your Message to the Masses, Turn Your Words into Wealth and Be a Book Business Boss." Julia is the author of 140+ books, published 400+, recorded 3 music CDs and coached others to be published authors and business owners. She is the owner of five companies, a non-profit organization and the editor of the Book Business Boss Magazine.

To stay connected with Julia, visit www.juliaakroyston.com.

Social Media

Facebook, Instagram, LinkedIN, TikTok and Threads - @juliaaroyston

X - @juliaakroyston

More Books by Julia A. Royston

Julia Royston Books
www.juliaroystonstore.com

Julia Royston Books
www.juliaroystonstore.com